SNARLS OF LOVE

By

Sandra Carvalho

NOTEBOOK|PUBLISHING

First published in the UK in 2014 by Notebook Publishing,
145–157 St John Street, London, EC1V 4PW.

www.notebookpublishing.co.uk

ISBN: 9780956553973

A CIP catalogue record for this book is available
from the British Library.

Typeset by Notebook Publishing.
Printed and bound in Great Britain.

DEDICATION

To my friend, gym buddy and jogging partner, Rhonda Ali: you never fail to brighten my days with your cheerful voice and jokes, which kept me up late at night, writing this book

To my Silent Women's Against Domestic Violence group: you are always in my thoughts and in my work.

To my sons, Adam and Simon, the tech guys: thank you for all of your support on this book.

We meet again
On the paths of time and mystery.
We meet again
As lovers as friends, as strangers.
Who knows...?
As we embrace our timeless love.
Fate.
Our future
Together or apart.

Sandra Carvalho

CHAPTER 1: WATER WARS

Malibu Canyon Park

'Damn it,' Judas paced the jogging trail of Canyon Park as the unforgiving July heat glared down on him, reminding him that he worked best in the winter when the air was ice and crisp. The cooler temperatures allowed him to at least stay alert long enough to carry out his assignment. He wished he could find a way to disappear into thin air.

Judas was a gifted soldier—one of two left: Jack Leb and Judas were allowed to live and travel freely, all in the name of the interest of the country's safety. They had no choice in the matter: they were gifted seers—especially trained in secret.

Judas had been discovered at the age of eleven, when he was living at the orphanage. A military special agent was in search of special young men, and the rest, as they say, is history. The lives of both Judas and Jack then became dedicated to the military, living in secrecy.

Jack became the perfect sniper.

Powerful corporations summoned Judas and Jack, with Jack's services in high demand in oil-rich and war-prone countries. Jack Leb, the Navy Seal-trained pilot and sniper, was regularly sent on overseas missions, the secrets of which were always kept confidential to the very last moment. But this life took its toll on Jack; fear of discovery can make a man turn on his very own family and society, which is exactly what happened to Jack. When he returned home after his final mission, his mind only knew how to respond to fear. He assaulted the bakery attendant with a hunter's knife because he thought he had been ignored by society. He knew he did not fit in anymore; he did not belong anywhere except on a battlefield or on assignment. Jack had become damaged goods.

The military waited for Jack either to commit suicide or die on a mission. They didn't want to dirty their hands.

The military was keeping the war business thriving with men like Jack Leb. He was home-grown: his Texas accent branded him; his significant height, gigantic size and towering body came from his Russian father; and, after his mother remarried and moved to Texas with his Mexican-American step-father, he learnt how to deal with people when the family opened a bed and breakfast inn. But the calm could not last, and soon the storm descended when Jack's stepfather put him out on the street at eleven years old. The reasons were unknown: military files showed no details.

The military kept Jack alive, but the other solider had a serial killer past. He had been recruited from one of the four hundred locked behind bars and taken to the military secret mental hospitals where experiments were carried out to improve gifted soldiers. Countless were trained as hybrid supernatural killers at secret locations to protect civilians form the terror plots that were increasing in number.

Judas impatiently glanced at his watch. He was not late for this job, but it was 11am and there had been no call. In his hands was the bio of Sara Stone, whose past was strikingly similar to his own: she was almost like a wanderer, chasing past ghosts and living out of an orphanage behind the White Chapel, living off the street. Her mentors had been some kind elderly nuns—and something about that touched him.

His boss was never this late giving him the green light, but now two hours had passed by and the job was supposed to be done...

Bang! Judas scrambled for cover as gunshots rang out from across the park next to the hiking trail. Judas watched as a woman emerged, her gun concealed inside her jacket. The initial moment of panic and the feeling of self-preservation were quickly replaced as Judas noticed her long, toned legs, perfectly balanced on her high heels, her fitted black jeans and floral top, which seductively revealed her olive skin. She was slender with jet-black curly hair that danced in the breeze, against her face, as she coolly walked away.

Judas sprang into action, knowing he could not lose her again. He tried to act fast, but the woman got into a black jeep. She smiled at Judas and blew him a kiss, inducing in him a shared memory; he recognised her. He knew he had known this mysterious but deadly woman during another time—but couldn't quite remember the night she spent with him when he was wounded.

Without much time to think, Judas grabbed her

arms. 'I know you…'

'And I know you,' Sara replied coldly as she glared at him, her forceful stare demanding her let her go. As not to alarm or scare her away, he did as her eyes suggested he should, and within them he recognised a deeper and darker world than his. He felt his heart crumble, her beautiful deep bronze eyes enticing him in. She was an exotic Arab-Asian mixed beauty with enticing beauty. His heart almost melted with the strong desire to steal her away from this place, which was soon about to be teaming with the cops.

As the hikers began gathering around a body not too far from where she emerged, she began to speak. 'I never did get your name that night… You disappeared on me.' Sara glanced over, locking eyes with her enemy.

Taking a deep breath, he studied her beautiful face: she was on the run—he could feel it—but she looked at him with a sad look and, without thinking, he quickly jumped into her jeep. She put her foot down on the accelerator and sped off. He did not attempt to stop her from leaving, knowing it would make him look weak.

His phone began to vibrate with the go-ahead code as curious hikers poured over the body of the mayor of Malibu, who had taken two bullet wounds to the head.

Summer Stag Party

The bodyguards at the Malibu Hotel, 'Hu'—the owner

and Native American 'Black Horse', and his daughter—
were old friends of Judas, and were the only two people
in the world he knew he could trust with his life.

'Black Horses come from a family of shamans
whose brothers were gifted with the ever-watching eyes
of the gods. Judas had been referred to as Wolf Spirit.
'You see my ancestors' ghosts? Something or someone
stirs your spirit... Come sit. Talk. What troubles your
mind other than your choice of job and your boss? I told
you evils would haunt your nights. You slept all day...
What keeps you up, my son?'

'That dream again... The devil keeps me awake.'
Judas rocked his head back and sat on the Indian woven
mat with a musing smile on his face. 'You know, you
smoke at night and now all the rooms smell of cigars.'

'That's funny, Wolf Spirit. Smoking is a way of
cleansing the house of bad wandering spirits. Now, you
speak about that dream...' Blackhorse said, his eyes
staring off into a faraway place. 'What dream?'

'How did you know about my dream?' Judas
replied.

'You just told me, my son.'

'Oh... Okay. I fear I am losing my mind now. I
need a vacation—a break from all this, from the blood
and death.' He began to smile. 'Do you think there is a
resort of some sort for my kind?' Judas asked
amusingly.

'No way, Wolf Spirit. Your resting place is amongst
the stars.' Black Horse pointed to the stars blanketing the
skies as they sat in the outdoor café.

'I believe in the teachings of the Buddha when it comes to reincarnation,' he joked. 'I believe I will return as a priest that performs miracles to cure terminally ill cancer patients. I am not sure why I feel this way, but I have been reading a lot about the life of the Buddha, Black Horse. I think it's time for me to find myself through something meaningful next time around. I know... I know what you're thinking... Come on, spit it out.' Smiling, Judas looked to Black Horse, whose eyes were closed. The cigar between his fingers fell to the ground. Judas slowly picked it up, and as he did he felt the strong hands of Black Horse holding his arms, softly speaking into his ears.

'Something big is coming your way.' Black Horse's voice was hoarse and throaty. 'Someone is coming—a woman who possesses the powers of the unseen worlds of the Gods. Her spirit is fearless. Death has given her his power to see where evil men roam. She is coming into your life, but you will have the answer you seek. Be strong for her. Trust her. Your dream is your guide to the doors of your destiny. Go with courage now.' Black Horse let go of Judas's arms. He stood and walked into the lobby.

Judas stood shaking. He did not want to kill the woman who could be the one.

Sometime later, the omen message still hadn't left Judas's mind; he felt he needed a beer and steamy hot sex to forget what he'd heard and to pass the time He returned to his hotel and called hotel services for a call girl. She was pretty, a slim Asian beauty with long black pencil-straight hair. Her makeup was heavy but he could see her beauty was deep and hauntingly untamed. He lay on the bed, waiting for her to get undressed, and when she had she crawled slowly upon him and unzipped his pants. His hard, hot, wet, throbbing dick was his master. He was the servant. He wanted to feel the warmth of a woman on fire, but for him, all he saw in his mind was her—Sara, a name he would never forget.

The way he called her name in his dream, he knew she was the only one that would save him from himself.

The dead silent of the night played with his mind, and his heart was on fire for her. His spirit thirsted for her touch, for him to know her, to protect her. Yet he knew: a name attached to a dream is as elusive as heaven would ever be to him, removing his pains and dark thoughts for only an hour. One blessed hour... What more could he ask of the devil? He already knew he had a special place in hell.

Black Horse was awakening with the burning of his flesh His feet and legs were on fire, his room engulfed in raging flame. Two men were in his room: one from his past, the other from his present—the latter being the developer who wanted to buy him out. They stood staring at him as the heat, the glassy flame, leapt towards his face.

And suddenly he woke and sat upright, like a dead man returning from the grave. His spirit could sense danger approaching.

He could feel his enemies edging closer. Judas could stick around long enough to protect his daughter, but his stepsister was coming to visit him—the one he had kept a secret from his daughter and the world. She had been gifted: he had to keep her a secret even from Judas, who he loved as a son. Judas had chosen his path a long time before he met him on his ranch, wounded and half-starved. With a tight grip on his gun, as though it was his best friend in the world, he had approached him before healing his wounds, which was miracle with the bullet lodged in his chest, close to his heart. Judas had been dying, yet he had lived through it. That night, the wolves had surrounded his ranch in respect of their own. They gave him the gift of their spirit, allowed him to live again, to serve their purpose.

Killing had come easy for Judas, his wolf nature earning him his name Wolf Spirit. But Black Horse knew Judas would find his place in this world with the woman that was born for him—the woman he was afraid may also be someone dear to his heart.

The spirits of the gods had spoken: they would protect her as they always had, for as long as she lived in this world.

Black Horse realised the importance of her work, and keeping her a secret was always the only way he could protect her. But Judas's dream troubled him, and his ancestors had spoken through him that night. He knew they were watching Judas, bringing them both together. If only James Stone was not the one calling the shots, Judas would be free to make his own decisions about his destiny. And he also knew Judas would be the only man that could protect her—and her work.

Of course, he knew the danger in their meetings, and James Stone had convinced them they could do anything to anyone at any time. He also knew there was a difference between the poor and the powerless, and the powerful: those in power can protect their own resources and family when the time comes around, whilst the poor cannot stand against the rich and powerful who put food on the table of their families and give them gifts to sell their resources—their land—where they, alone, can profit. The poor are cursed and blessed with ignorance, the rich preserving their lives whilst stealing their life supply through their land. This could be seen widely, with the water war breaking down the lives of many in Brazil, the struggles of those in the country being broadcast across the news every hour, taking the form of riots.

'This is bad for business,' Black Horse said to his manager as he sipped his morning coffee. 'My guests come in from Brazil. It looks bad. The army has moved in. The water protesters are not backing out. There are reports of daily beatings on the streets of San Paulo.'

The town was where the water reservoir had been discovered and where the locals had enjoyed free access. But now the river had been blocked off by electricity-wired fence, with local children dying as a result of trying to get across. Countless had been killed instantly as deadly bolts of current had passed through their helpless bodies. The locals were screaming murder as a result of being left thirsty for days. They had been forced into poverty, and now had no choice but to arm themselves and be ready to fight back to preserve their God-given resources.

The fights had spilt out onto the streets, and there had been the clashes of the police and the locals, which caused chaos amongst the international media and the West, with Human Rights groups visiting the small town in an effort to make peace. However, the news reports and awareness campaigns had faded into the background, drowned out by the latest news coming from Syria, where women were raped and tortured.

'Damn news… It's always bad these days.'

Judas was in pain. He needed to know who Sara was, if she existed, and whether she was *his*—the one for him. He was sure his mind was slipping away, tangled around Sara, the woman he could not be with because she existed only in his dreams. On the other hand, could it have been as Black Horse predicted? He was always so good at knowing things invisible to the naked eye.

Black Horse worked three days at the inn and two days as an Insurance Investigator at the Malibu Insurance Firm, whose clients were the elite rich and newly famous young millionaires. Recently, five young Silicon Valley investors had been killed in their vacation homes in the Philippines. All five were meeting stakeholders in a bid to sell out their shares, with word on the news detailing that all had died from bullet wounds to the head during the course of meetings. The murderer was speculated as having been part of meetings that went sour, but the killer had, in each case, left a note, reading *Find me. Catch me if you dare*.

The news reported that the killers (or even a lone killer) were visiting Malibu and, in the days that followed, were assigned a job resembling that of a killing spree. A total blackout had occurred in the haunted city of Malibu and, through the darkness, a hooded figure, with hands in pockets—potentially a homeless man looking to steal a bit of cash or maybe someone far more dangerous—stalked out his victim.

'You've got to tell me why Black Horse is protecting this woman... From who? From what? Who is she, Job? If you know something, man, I ain't got the time for mystery games.'

'Don't ask. Look, you wouldn't believe it. Think she is the one, you know. She is your secret informant. She was the one that saved you from a bullet. It had your name written on it, man. And now she's brought you back here to finish the job. *You* are the job, Judas,' Job said as he turned to face his computer screen.

'She wants to be found,' Judas replied calmly. 'She wants to die. Why would she hire someone to kill her? It would make sense if she was a coward, but she isn't. You should have seen her. A man was killed in cold blood, and she walked away coolly like she'd done it a million times before.' He stalked away, out of sight from the lobby, telling himself he desperately needed a break from this work. And it was then, with images of beaches and relaxation dancing across his mind—thoughts of a real vacation, not like being sent overseas on contracts, but something real where work never called and when he wasn't always looking over his shoulder—that loud explosives rang out in the direction of the car park.

Judas rushed towards the balls of fire and thick black smoke as it began quickly engulfing the Malibu evening sky over the car park. From a distance, someone was screaming for help—a woman with broken glasses and blood running down the side of her head, pouring from a deep wound on her temple, a piece of broken glass deeply embedded. The woman was walking around in circles, screaming out the name Marcus, her blood-soaked blouse telling the tale of her trauma. Judas moved in to help her, and as he got closer, something told him he knew this woman. Amidst the blood and the chaos, the screaming and fright, memories flashed through his mind her face staring down at him asleep in some other place, some other time.

CHAPTER 2: TERROR PLOTS

'Help me! My son is in that car! Please!' The woman's pleads and screams came as she helplessly held on to Judas's arms. Judas ran towards the black Honda, which was now engulfed in flames. It was too late: the flames engulfed the car.

Judas felt overwhelmed with emotion—a trait unfamiliar to him, his years spent on secret missions removing his capacity to feel. But as tears pricked, he made eye contact with the young man, who smiled wickedly at Judas. His emotion evaporated, and Judas felt chills run down his spine as he adjusted his thoughts, trying to think clearly enough to understand what was happening outside the Black Horse hotel. He needed answers—and the woman, now being treated by an ambulance crew—was going to give them to him. He would not let her get away this time, and if she were responsible for the explosions, they would have to answer to him. This was getting personal—and too close for comfort.

Judas watched as the woman and her son received treatment for their wounds. Judas felt stalked and targeted. His thoughts whirred and questions probed, and just as he made the decision to head over to the ambulance and begin his investigation, the ambulance doors slammed shut.

Judas ran towards the vehicle, calling out to the medics to stop but to no avail. They sped off, carrying with them the woman, whose life could easily be in danger, and her son. Judas hurriedly got into a cab, demanding the driver follow the ambulance. His chest was tight, and it was then that he felt a sudden sharp pain that lingered and plucked at his heart. The sensation was strange, and then came a sharp pain to his forehead as if he had been stabbed forcefully with a sharp object. He closed his eyes and, when he reopened them, he saw her looking down at him—her face bloody—yet she was nowhere in the cab. Judas pulled himself from his dream, feeling like he had lost a lot of time when, in fact, he was still following the ambulance.

'Hey, man, can you tell me if I fell asleep?' he asked the cab driver.

With a slight puzzled look on his face, the driver, in a heavy Indian accent, responded, 'Yeah, you did, actually. You were calling a woman's name.' He eyed him suspiciously from the rear-view mirror, looking at him through narrowed eyes. 'Are you alright, man? My name is Ali. What's yours?'

'Yeah... I'm okay, thanks for asking. What did you say your name was again?'

'Ali... I told you just a moment ago. I guess you can't hear so well. No wonder after that explosion back at the hotel. Everyone is on the street here, nervous. You never know who or where their next target will be, you know. Every time this shit happens, names like mine go back on the blacklist as though every person carrying the name *Ali* is responsible for every bloody bombing attack, you know what I mean, man? I am a potential victim here as well, working my ass off to pay my rent. Every cab driver like me is targeted by racial gangs on the streets, and I'm fed up of this shit.' He shook his head in frustration. 'Don't mind me. I'm just venting my anger. You see, there's a cop who works the night shift around here, and word on the street is he is the leader of a White racist group. And, talk of the devil, he is heading right for us.' The cab driver turned to Judas. 'I've got to slow down, man, he is on us. Can't follow the ambulance anymore. I've got to let you out here. Don't want any trouble, you understand.'

Judas smiled. 'No problem. Let me out here, but first let me thank you.' Judas paid the driver extra. As he walked away, he pulled out his gun and aimed it at the cab driver. He shot him in the back of his head, his brain splattering across the car's windows. Putting the gun back in his jacket pocket, he got a phone call from another green light job, just as a text flashed up on his screen. *Shoot the bloody Indian cab driver if he is disturbing your peace… That was a joke!*

There had been a time when Judas did not need an explanation for his green light. He was told to kill and so he did, but now something had changed: he wanted deeper answers and reasons. Now it had to involve something more—and the reason behind that was the woman who had saved his life. She had tended to his wounds in a cabin in the woods when he had been left to die out in the cold. But there was something more complex: she had a role in all of this, he knew, but Black Horse had the answers to his questions because he knew her.

But he knew: she was his stepsister, the one Blackhorse Black Horse had always kept a secret. She was the Seer Detective woman and Crime Writer—only she wasn't here for a book tour. This was why she was caught in between the devil and the dark blue sea; she was the target but she was a moving target—and she knew her enemies. A former pastry chef from the White House wanted her dead, and he was linked to a notorious drug cartel from Mexico. With links in Arizona and Malibu, the trade routes were under attack—and who knows what deadly attack would await Judas.

The time on Judas's watch stopped at 11:11—when they had given Judas the green light. *Get the job done ASAP.*

Everybody is valuable at some time or another. Hell, even gardeners for rich people have a price put on their heads; they know more about their employer's dark secrets and ins and outs than the bloody cops. They make my work easy, And it was with this thought that Judas was starting to believe that gardeners could be groomed into Pro Assassins, although whether or not they would survive after 'one kill' would be another matter.

It's easiest to kill when you are trained and when you make it your career, but, as with all careers, a vacation away was needed sometimes.

Judas, in spite of his profession, had normal dreams and hopes. He wanted to fall in love, and he realised that, if he was ever going to, it would be with the mysterious woman that took care of him after he stumbled onto her porch six months before in that small town called Blackwood valley heights—his escape route though the California Redwood Forest. His last kill was a married man on a sightseeing trip with his outside mistress. Judas had ended their planned future skiing trip to Alaska—almost a happy ending. In the fall, Judas had spared his mistress, who was a casino owner's daughter. Her father wanted his daughter's relationship to end, and he was not waiting to see things go wrong for his only daughter. Judas took his daughter home; she never saw the face under the ski mask. She was in shock, but she knew her father's reputation and his dealings. Melissa Weans knew this to be her dad's work: he was the only one who knew where she had been.

Melissa had made the classic mistake of falling in love with a married man. John had been sneaking around for over a year. He said he was planning on getting a divorce, but he was a heavy gambler at her dad's casino, and his debts were high at the time he left with her. But she had fallen in love with him. He was fun to be around, he took care of her bills, and he was an accountant for her dad.

With the truth coming out, Melissa had become thirsty for revenge: she wanted her dad dead. She hadn't ever expected it to go this way, but the twenty million in the vaults meant her father's casino was doing well, even in the economic downturn. John was a means to an end and a way of getting the money she rightfully deserved.

~*~*~*~

Melissa walked lovingly into the arms of her brother Teddy Weans, who was off duty from the Syria war. A Navy pilot, Ted was Melissa's support, and he planned the match with the married man.

'Oh, how is my baby girl sis?' he said sweetly, kissing her on the lips.

'Great. I missed you.'

Melissa's quiet reply worried him.

Behind closed doors, they were a couple. Both were bisexual, so it made no difference in their world as they both had only each other—and that was all that mattered. Their mother had died when they were teenagers, their father was a womaniser who loved to have men over and partake in group sex, especially with those in their 20s. Melissa had hated men from then on, but now she wanted to give it all up to be with her brother and girlfriends; living away from it all.

The memory of their mother kept her and Teddy together.

Teddy grabbed her up like a ragdoll and spun her around. She was tall and muscular, his tan skin making him look like an Arab. 'Take me home, girl. Don't look like that... Aren't you glad to see me? I'm here now. Everything is going to be alright. I will take care of things from now on. The only thing is *he* will be seeing us. Trust me, sis, this guy I hired is good. They call him the *Judas* of all traitors. He does the job clean and he moves on. His fees are high but it comes with the danger

26

of the job and because he was a solider—US Special Seal Unit team. The army let him go when he got his best friend and comrade killed in the line of fire, disobeying orders from his sergeant.'

'Really?' she questioned. 'That sounds awful.'

'There's a lot more to it, sis. It was too dark for him to see or save his friend, but an enemy sniper from the Muslim brotherhood fighters for Islam killed his friend. No one knows where the shot came from. Judas fought hard to save his friend's life that day. The Syrian dust settled on his friend as he fell to the ground. He's said to be broken and bruised inside. Judas, they say, is a man living with his demons on his back—or, in this case, taking revenge for his friend through his work. Darkness like that never leaves, baby. It will never leave him alone. It finds its way even in sleep through inner screams at recurring nightmares. His late-night sweats. His dark corners will reveal where his mind wanders.'

'He sounds completely tortured.'

'I'm sure it doesn't all come down to that, though. No one really knows where he came from. His parents are unknown, as well as his country of origin. His files read like a mystery novel. His accent doesn't betray him as he is trained to speak with both British and American accents depending on the country of his work. His acting skills and voice training hold his secrets.'

~*~*~*~

Driving into Melissa's father's driveway, leading up to

his sprawling tri-level mansion, she could see her dad was home early. They expected he would be waiting on them. Melissa was the first to knock on the door, which eerily opened slightly on its own. Melissa peered inside and, there on the floor, was a blood trail leading to the kitchen and into the pool area. Moments later they found their father head-down in the pool, wearing his suit from the casino. He had bullet wounds in his arms and at the back of his head.

Melissa's scream rang out as she held onto Teddy, who wore nothing but a scorned and remorseful look of satisfaction on his face. 'The job was done,' he whispered to Melissa as the emergency medic cops arrived. It was then that the fake tears came fast. Melissa and Teddy kept it real, depicting a touching scene of the grieving son and daughter.

The detectives asked a couple of questions, but nothing pointed to any motives. Melissa and Teddy stuck to their story about visiting their dad to celebrate his birthday.

Judas was taken aback by the news of the well-known casino owner's death as he had not known the man was popular or well-known in the community, particularly for his philanthropic activities and donations to charities. Maybe it was down to him doing two jobs on the same day that caused such emotions; usually, he did not do double killings on the same day, but the client was a Navy Officer from a US Warship who was in town and wanted the job done on the same day.

Judas had wanted to get out of town as soon as the

job was done. He fled to Malibu that same night, and that was where he got into the accident, when Sara found him unconscious in his car, bleeding from a deep gushing wound to his head. He begged her not to take him to a hospital, so she took him home, trusting him with her life. That stormy night, when he awoke in the cabin, he saw an angel of light with a sad look on her face. It was love he felt instantly in his heart. She was divine, and he wanted to hold on to her and never let her go. Had his arms not been bandaged and the pain unbearable, he would have held on to her as tightly as he could.

CHAPTER 3: SEER INVESTIGATORS

Sara was rushing out the door when she remembered she had an injured man in her guest bedroom—and his name was Judas. The name was on the file given to her by someone dear to her heart: her stepdad, Blackhorse.

Her biological father was American Indian, and he owned and ran a hotel on the outskirts of Malibu's coastal bay area, where surfers would frequently stay overnight.

Sara was being recognised as an esteemed author: her new detective book, *Dark World*, which centred on missing children and teens—cold cases, in particular—was doing well at the local Indie bookstore. It was climbing the Bestsellers list—fast and furiously.

Sara's day job was to find missing children. She was a gifted seer private investigator she was known to have an instinct that could lead her to a missing child without looking at the child's photo she could see the invisible world where murderers live or commit their crimes where time doesn't exist. She could go and look back into the crime, see how it happened, and find the location. She had travelled far and wide—even as a child—to find others with her gift.

Making money from a gift like this was a bonus, but seeing someone die—knowing where and who had killed that person—tired the mind, making it wary of seeing too much darkness of the human soul.

Sara opened the bedroom door and saw Judas

standing against the window, deep in thought. He looked like a broken toy solider, his arms bandaged, his jet-black hair creating an air of mystery. 'I see you made it to the bathroom.'

Judas looked at her with a puzzled look and, as if her breath-taking beauty instantly possessed him, he slowly limped towards her petite frame. Standing before her for a moment, their eyes locked. He suddenly pulled her towards him with his uninjured hand and kissed her long and passionately.

In that moment, Sara could feel his longing to be hers. His kiss and his mind were now hers, as was his body. Instantly, she struggled like a live doll against his chiselled chest while he took her in his arms, breathing in her hair and its sweet morocco oil.

In his deep, throaty voice, Judas forced her name from her lips. 'Sara, is that your name? I heard it on your answering machine.' He looked at her, suddenly aware that he'd kissed her without any indication she'd wanted him to. 'That was a *thank you* kiss. I know women who pick up wounded men at night—women such as you—who want a man to kiss them like that,' he commented with a wink, his hard eyes now smiling playfully and wickedly.

Judas went into the bathroom and Sara, now fuming, followed him.

'Oh yeah? Well, whatever your name is, maybe you go around leaving people on the roadside to die from their gunshot wounds. You are lucky it was me that found you. And I'm not like those women you hook up with!' She marched out of the room, angry and shaken by the mere presence of this man who she had taken a gamble on by bringing him to her hideaway—a place only two people knew about. She should have known from his musky scent and unshaven look—his unkempt yet rough but also sexy face—and by his bold passionate spirit that she should run. But he made her feel safe. 'It's a rare thing these days to trust too much, you know,' she yelled. 'You could get yourself killed. Or worse, you could lose your mind!'

Judas yelled back. 'What the hell, woman? Are you cop or a lawyer? I'm not a fugitive on the run! At least, the last time I checked you were the one that had chosen to pick me up!' He rolled his eyes towards the ceiling, shaking his head. He felt compelled to give in to this strange woman who, by the look of things, lived alone and who seemed sadly lonely. But soon, he thought to himself, he would have her wrapped around his little finger and have her begging for it.

With exasperation, he pulled his fingers through his hair. 'Okay, okay. How about we introduce ourselves properly? But I suggest you join me for a bath... If you want to fight, we could do it in there together. That would be more fun! Oh, and by the way, my name is Judas... I hope that makes you less angry with me.'

The bang of the bedroom door being slammed shut was the response, which caused him to smile broadly with pleasure. He liked this woman: she awakened an inner heat in him and made him feel safe to let down his guard, which was the first time he'd felt like that since being sixteen when he'd had to leave his sick dad, who was a great detective from the NYPD.

His mother was to blame for his distrust of women and their lack of compassion, as his mother had taken him from his dad. His dad had lost his mind: he had begun seeing things, hallucinating, imagining people that were not visible to him or anyone else around him. His mother had loved his dad but she came from a rich family who insisted she leave him. When she did, she died in a car accident—just as his dad had said she would. Since that fatal day, Judas had known life was unforgiving—just like God—and so he chose to trust only his instincts and never his heart.

Sara responded just as he wanted, but, despite the humour, he felt this woman could somehow fill the void that life had created through robbing him of the one thing he'd missed out on. That one thing that had the potential to make men kill, go mad, and be willingly to die for. That one thing would be a lot more dangerous than the man he had become—and it was that he feared so much. It was as dangerous and ruthless and selfish as he was.

Judas closed his eyes in thought before walking out towards the street of hell once again. He fclt he belonged now. He felt something, although he wasn't sure what he felt. Whatever it was, it pulled him forward like he was flying rapidly though a black hole—taking him with her.

The scent of her hit him. That was his heart claiming its right to be alive in this universe. His place was next to her.

Judas left the next day. He never again saw her until that morning in the park. He knew something was wrong; she was a mysterious woman with deep secrets, secrets she would take to her grave, yet he wanted to know everything about her. His heart had raced when she was in the room. Maybe he was losing his touch. Maybe he was beginning to show remorse for his prey— or maybe just this one.

'So you're telling me there are inter-dimensional earth worlds, and the whole damn universe is a hoax or a hologram designed to fool the human eye, all looking right back at us? There are aliens or gods, hybrid advanced beings, us of the future, laughing at us as they watch us, like we're in some kind of comedy show?' Sara sarcastically asked her friend Judith at their weekly coffee meet, which would usually involve a book talk and other news.

'Girl, I don't know how and why you bother with the scientific world of make-believe. For God's sake, who can know for sure why anything exists on earth or out there? The whole damn thing is a big mystery to keep us from getting bored to death,' Judith's said as she sipped on her coffee.

'Yeah, well, right now the mystery that needs to be solved is how you can speak with a mouth full of éclairs! Wow, Judith, now *that* is a mystery!' At first laughing aloud, Sara then went silent and looked ahead into the distance, searching miles away where a hooded young man was jogging along the side of the road before stopping at a coffee shop.

She could sense danger approaching.

Instantly, she was standing in the coffee shop. Looking around, she saw the strange tall hooded jogger enter before shooting the cashier and then opening his hoody and exposing a jacket wired with a bomb, which thankfully never did go off. He tried and struggled with the jacket but, as he struggled, his gun went off. The jogger shot himself in the forehead, causing blood to splatter across Sara's face. She frantically wiped her cheeks.

Sara's puzzled expression alarmed Judith. 'What's wrong?

'He's there after us. Just stay close.' Sara pulled Judith her out of the chair and told her to run. They both ran next door and breathlessly entered the car park next to the coffee shop, only the young bomber had gone. He walked out coolly, crossing the street before entering the hair salon next door. Mere seconds later, there were short screams and shouts, together with a loud explosion, as a bomb went off inside the salon.

Sara's perceptions were never this wrong—unless the bomber was gifted and could sense her presence and divert his original target. The terrorists were evolving: they were being groomed and trained in their hate crime right here amongst their leaders.

Despite the bomber's bloody crimes, however, Sara had seen in his eyes a flicker of hurt and pain as he had glanced momentarily to the orphanage shelter across the street. He had been thrown out onto the street, left for the wolves, when he had told his mother he could speak to spirits. He had been gifted as a child; he could see the human spirit, the soul, as it departed the body. He could see how they would die. But his gift was feared, and his mother deserted him, abandoning him onto the street at just 14 years old, at which point he was forced to go to the orphanage to shelter—until he decided to take Fate into his hands. That was his story the—only one he was supposed to remember.

Sara recalled where she met him: it was at her last book signing. He read the first chapter, and was anxious and impatient to get out of there—until she touched his hands and looked into his eyes as she signed his copy of her latest detective terrorist crime non-fiction. He had pulled away and ran out of the store, mumbling under his breath in Arabic. Sara knew he had been brainwashed by professed, selfish, religious men with an evil agenda, who had preached and targeted young valuable minds— just like Jake Walker. Without question, he was looking for acceptance in the wrong place, yet it felt right to him, and he wanted to leave his mark. He had done that today. His name would go down in history. He would become known as the Malibu Bomber.

'Sara, how did you know? Did the cops tip you off? I'm confused.' Judith's worried face interrupted Sara's thoughts. Her expression showed stress and shock as she continued to question what had just happened.

'He bombed the wrong location, Judith,' Sara

explained in an anxious tone 'It was supposed to be the coffee shop. But he knew I would not have died in there. They will send more after him… Don't forget my words. I am marked for death, Judith. I have to get you home. We've not got much time. You're not safe with me anywhere.' Sara took a deep breath and hurried quickly to her friend, telling her to leave now. She walked Judith to the car. She took out her mobile phone and called her old detective friend, but he did not answer the phone, which was disturbing to her. Deeply dark and disturbed minds gather into one place to do evil to harm and kill happy people. Angry people live to torment them—the happier folk—like they are too self-absorbed to notice the fire of icy, all-consuming grudges that fester in silent hate.

Events from her last book were eerily breathing into horrific and very real events here. Why did Jake Walker do what he had done?

Sara called her partner and old detective friend, Howard Cooper. She paced nervously around her home office space, barefooted, stubbing her toes on her office chair and folding her arms impatiently as she listened to his deep, gravel voice raise higher and higher.

'Why the hell do you think he did it, Sara? It's all over the bloody news! Put on your TV and calm down. No one is after you. Jake was romantically involved with a hairstylist at that salon before he joined the terrorist cell group. He must be secretly fighting his sexual urges and he's losing that battle. That reached an all-time low when he saw his lover with the owner of the salon—she was making out at his lover's place! He got into an argument with the guy, and his boss—the owner—fired Jake right there on the spot—at least, that's what his teary-eyed, sobbing lover told us when we contacted him. He told us Jake had links with the Taliban, and he had encouraged him to attend meetings and even tried to recruit him, but he said he had to get a restraining order against him. Apparently, the last thing Jake told him was that he'd take them all to hellfire where they belonged.'

'Intense. Really intense,' Sara said anxiously.

'Insane world, right?' Howard, excited about the source that had given him inside intel, continued. 'He said he thought it was just an idle threat and that he hadn't expected him to do anything like this... But don't they all? Jake, however, was a closet gay, and he felt his only way out was through the terrorist cell brotherhood.' Coughing and clearing his throat, Detective Cooper then fell deadly silent.

The sniper bullet did not miss its target.

Sara felt a sickening feeling sweep over her, feeling like something was deadly wrong. Suddenly, she saw herself standing next to Detective Cooper's body on the floor, a fatal gunshot wound to his head. His blood was splattered across his daughter's wedding photo, which sat neatly and otherwise untouched next to his desk. There had been no struggle: the killer was a sniper, and the bullet had travelled through Cooper's study window, hitting him as he had sat at his desk. Sara knew the killer bullet had been ejected from a sniper military rifle.

She looked across towards the broken glass as it

happened, and had watched as the bullet slowly flew by her, entering the side of her friend's temple, killing him instantly as he slumped to the floor clutch. In his palms was a note for Sara: *His name is Ju...* The pen had slipped from his hands before he could finish.

Sara could see the killer in her mind: she would never forget his cold, penetrating eyes staring into hers as he aimed his rifle at her faithful old friend and investigating crime partner. Sara blinked, trying to show courage and not tears. They had both worked together, solving high-profile kidnap cases together, working in secret and saving lives from being destroyed at the hands of killers just like Judas. She knew they had met somewhere before. She'd saved his life—yet he'd killed her partner.

Sara, weakened by her emotion and grief, fell to her knees and sobbed uncontrollably. Cooper had been the only other person she had wanted and could have trusted, although recently she had felt he'd been hiding something from her. He had avoided working on any more cases. She had thought he wanted out and had left it there, but he had always seemed to know when she had found the killer. She wanted to listen to heart—not to her instincts. She wanted to remember her old friend as he had been.

Suddenly, she was pulled back into her body. Sensation tingled though her body, reminding her that she was back from witnessing the murder of her friend. Feeling how dry her throat was, she went for a glass of water.

Judas's face was etched on her mind.

Sara realised something had been wrong with her visions. Her vision of Jake Walker had been wrong; he hadn't detonated the bomb in the coffee shop. Sara knew that sometimes her visions became confused, like seeking someone out in a crowd, and it wasn't long after the Jake Walker incident that a man had walked into the coffee shop and shot the cashier; his wife, who he had discovered had been cheating on him.

Despite the frustrations, being wrong was sometimes good with her gift: she never wanted to be right about seeing it happen. In fact, she hoped none of it was real. Sara thought she would wake up and it would all go away, but she knew deep down this would not be the case. She felt fear as a chill ran down her spine, like a bolt of lightning had struck. It felt like tiny pins had pricked across her entire body. And with that sensation, she was certain of something: she knew the killer was stalking her.

CHAPTER 4: SARA—PRISON

Someone was at her back door or in the garden. She could sense Mala was in danger, but she could not see where or how... Someone's thoughts were blocking hers.

Sara had left the door open when she went out to water her rose garden. Her assistant, Mala Gobi from India Major in Ancient Historian Arts and Artefacts, was young and brilliant. The two had met at Sara's yoga class, and they had both connected instantly. Of course, Mala was gifted: she was clairvoyant and could also tell your future by reading your palm. But now her cold body lay still, her blood still warm. Her killer was close. He had shot Mala from behind, at close range, with a silencer. She had been caught off-guard and had no chance of defence.

This killer seemed to know she would sense him— but how could he in Sara's rose garden?

Her assistant was dead. Her blood soaked the very soil she had brought for Sara the day before, telling Sara that, the darker the soil, the more fertile it would be. She was always quick to point out the significance of the history behind everything, which sometimes was annoying, but Sara quickly learned things from Mala; various helpful tips for her novels. Mala told her that the colour 'black' means 'futile' but 'fruitful' to the Arab world. But now she was dead. Murdered.

Her friend and assistant were gone.

Mala's eyes showed the surprise and fear of her killer's attach. She had been shot from behind, the bullet clearly killing her instantly.

Sara recognised one thing: everyone she knew or worked with were dropping like flies. Nonetheless, she did not have the answer, and her mind and visions were not as accurate as they had been in the past. She was working on a particular case in 2011—an abduction case of a child bride who died at the hands of an Arab prince a child had been found dead, hanging from her bedroom the day after she was handed over to her soon-to-be-husband. Sara was hired to find her: the little girl had been the daughter of a close friend from the women's group she had helped form in Yemen.

Her next assignment with the company reminded her of the presence of the killer who was stalking her from every corner now... It was personal. The killer silently stalking her meant she would need to cancel her assignment with the company that had hired her to work on a special case. She had been asked to establish the whereabouts of an ex-marine. Her instincts had told her to gain his trust, but now the case felt wrong. Instead, Sara would need to travel inside the dark, twisted mind of her stalker—and her head reeled with fear at the frightful thoughts. It was like peering through time: Sara was transported back to witness the horrific killings by a hired sniper, his masked face revealing only his deep amber, magnetic eyes in her memory, his soul lost somewhere inside of his guilt. Something told her she had met this man before, but she could not be sure if her visions were, once again, playing tricks with her mind.

With her mind overloading and her breathing becoming erratic, Sara realised she needed space to think, to consider what the visions could really mean. She was not about to let it go: she needed to know whether Judas, the man she saved a couple months ago, the injured stranger who touched every nerve in her body, compelling her to trust him and do as he said—even though she had known he was on the run from his past—was involved. But before then, she needed to say goodbye to her friend.

She held Mala in her arms and sobbed uncontrollably. Her friend's life had been cut so short, and it felt almost like nothing could have prevented it.

She felt desperate. Her memory recalled the times pursuing the cases of missing children, when she'd raced against the clock to save their lives before it was too late. But that was five years ago, when she was away from the lovely coastal town and in the dark inner city of New York where everyone and everything was not what it seemed; where the back alleys housed young men, waiting for bright, shining limos to pull up and take them for a ride, where they would work their magic of sex for money, their young bodies delighting the rich men. They paid well—business was good in the dark back alleys of New York, which where Sara's job had led her. She needed to take out the owner of a company who sold young men to older rich men; a disgusting creature who would lure the men into his limo, with the prey then disappearing from the streets of New York.

Sara did her job well: she saw the outcome before it happened. Nothing was hidden to her; she was guided to her next mission by an unseen force, using her intel and her trusted information and detailed visions on special cases. She had been trained well by the FBI and Interpol, with both organisations watching and targeting her from being a child, recognising her gift. They watched from a distance, analysing her gift after it came to light following her dad's murder by a special unit force. The murder had been carried out as a result of him knowing 'too much'; there were dirty cops and dirty agents who wanted him dead, who would do what was necessary to keep their cover intact. And so, after being approached, Sara chose to fulfil her destiny and work for them, helping her hometown in the process.

She had established a life, built a career that had been full of horror but also achievement when helping to bring about justice. And she had a navy pilot boyfriend. Life had been good, but her boyfriend had not returned home one day. He had gone missing, his journal detailing hidden events surrounding the sex trade and the kidnapping of young Asian teenage girls. He detailed where they were hidden, with some of them shot by soldiers when they tried to escape their fate. The girls' home village had been scarce of water, with the springs off-limits to the poor villages; water had been greedily bottled and sold by giant, foreign water companies. The journal detailed the killing of three young teenagers at a base that was covered up the US and Russian Military. Sara knew he must have disappeared for reasons

44

unknown to her, but she received a letter, which, although brief, gave her some answers, scribbled in his rough, wild handwriting:

Sara,

When next we meet, it will not be in this world. They are getting closer, and I am tired of running. My best friend is a skilled sniper and has a zany humorous personality. He will not harm you unless he is paid to do so; it's about the rush he gets from every paid kill. His revengeful black heart is alive for that sole purpose. He was a sole survivor of two fatal plane crashes, with 300 passengers killed. He walked away unscathed: he was on a mission to kill his target, who was a victim on-board. He was supposed to kill him on his way to the cab outside the airport, but some great force from above was doing his job that day—or so he told me in his letters. Now, they are in your hands, located inside the journal. Be aware of him: you can tame him with your charm and your mystical gifted mind. You know what to do to revenge my death, Sara. I will always love you, but don't ever lose your guard around him. He is a charmer.

But, like all men, he has a weakness: he loves to pay for sex from young Asian petite ladies. He loves to hear them scream. Rough sex helps him to get off, especially when they say it hurts. I am telling you all of this because I am sitting here right now looking at him as he holds a gun to my head; he is telling me to write about him, as one friend to another.

It's important you know, Sara, that I would rather

die at his hands than at his boss's—or whoever put the hit on me. He was recently relieved from his duties—he snapped and killed his Sargent—and I had to report it. Since then, I've been his enemy and friend, but today he knows he is going to kill his friend, the man you love and who loves you. I always will.

Follow your heart and he will protect you. He was a good man once upon a time, but now he lives for revenge. I asked him to find you and protect you. I do hope he opens up the Bible I sent him. I am sure he has not, but something tells me your paths will cross. He is a cold-stone killer, and the army has abandoned him so now his wreath is upon the innocents as well as the guilty. Now, he is a paid hit man for a specific company, and he goes by the name of Judas.

Again, I am sorry for abandoning you, but I must do so to keep you alive.

Sara sobbed silently, tears streaming, her heart feeling like it had been ripped apart as her fears grew alongside her anger. His name alone made her angry. She had him close enough and off-guard enough to put his light out, to rid this world from yet another raging madman that could easily become a spree killer or a bomber—or worse. But now he could be on her trail.

Taking a deep breath, Sarah knew she would never be able to identify his location if she did not relax, close her eyes, and meditate; trying to actively focus on where he was, using her natural vision. Although the gaps meant they were not always accurate, she knew she could achieve what she needed to—if she focused enough. On the other hand, however, if the person she wanted to see also shared her gift—and she knew of a couple of madman rapist killers that were aware of this gift—they could use it to harm others and block her out totally, like casting a dark veil over her vision, closing her mental eyes, allowing her to see only the darkness of their actions but not where they were. This, however, was only possible when they were aware of her looking for them.

Sara was quite sure Judas did not have the power; she felt nothing of it when she met him. But she also realised there was also the possibility of him totally blocking her out. She was also learning that she did not know much about others with the gift and how they communicate; nevertheless, following the events of the Muslim gay lover who became a bomber, she was learning quickly. At any time, tracking the location of Judas would be at the top of her agenda, and everything else would have to wait—even the case she was working on: solving the death of the man who was about to become her husband.

Sarah had felt, right from the moment people found out about her gift (*curse* she thought was a more appropriate name), that she was living in a prison.

Looking ahead, Sarah knew loneliness would seep into her aching but shapely body, and she would find herself waiting for him when he returned from a fresh kill. A great sadness rested on her chest as she closed her eyes and saw him sitting at the café, wolfing down his grilled spicy chicken pitta bread sandwich. She heard his phone ring, and he answered with a full mouth and an annoyed tone. 'What the fuck is wrong, man? Didn't I tell you not to call this fucking number unless I tell you? Just keep your eyes on the target and wait for my call! What's the matter with you? Wetting your panties if you mess up! I will kill you, okay?' Judas's curled lips bit mockingly with a twisted and smirked smile as he hung up, slamming the phone onto the rustic stone coffee table as he turned his head slowly. Sara saw his eyes staring into hers, causing her to feel a jolt, a fiery shockwave like a vortex of emotion, stealing her mind as he peered into her. She released his invisible but powerful hold over her body and emotions; as a woman, she was reminded of his dark attractive maleness pulling her closer to him, even if she was nowhere near where he was. Somehow, she knew he realised she was seeing where he was sitting. She had to find out everything about his secrets, about his hidden powers, and how he knew how to lure her in.

CHAPTER 5: SMOKELESS FIRE

Judas's smouldering body, ripped, muscular chest, and olive skin all came together to heat up the Malibu coastal beach. He sauntered across the beach, flipping away the sand from his shorts, revealing his lean torso, making him look like the Grand Canyon on fire in the summer time. This was one of the most breath-taking views along the rugged remote beauty of the Malibu coastal beach.

He would notice her, clad in a seductive drop-dead two-piece black-and-white-checked bikini, her long sensual legs attracting the most dangerous dark.

Suddenly, gunshots fired out from a hidden location. Bullets snarled past as he dived down on the beach, pinned her under him. She felt his body against her, the sand grating her skin, but the red-blooded man still inducing in her the deepest sexual desires. He took her in his arms like a live ragdoll as she clung to his muscular arms, overwhelmed by his closeness that threatened to yank the perimeter surrounding her heart, causing her to feel tangled by his throbbing heart.

The deafening noise and the power of the blast caused Sara to scream with rage and fear. She struggled to break free, sinking her teeth into his arms. He smirked before allowing himself to break into a broad smile, looking down at her bite mark in his arms.

'You can turn me on later. Now's not a good time,' he smiled. 'I need you to trust me right now—and *don't* fight me! It will only tire you out.' Judas lightly kissed her ear before grabbing her throat slowly and dragging her to her feet. His eyes flicked, like a light bulb fighting for energy, and a fire began to burn in his eyes; fire for the body he held clasped against his own. He took her mouth roughly and passionately, causing her body to weaken and feel like jelly. Her heart felt like she was about to die—either as the result of a heart attack or a broken heart.

He was so alone he had excluded himself from the human species...

His thoughts shot though her mind. His dark, brutally cruel nature, his sexy arms, his piercing eyes, his tongue devouring her mouth like a hungry lover... Boundaries... He knew how to break a woman's heart, but she wondered if she would give hers to him willingly. She knew she had to do more than pretend it was for real; she had to show him trust enough.

She pulled away and saw Judas was trying to distract the two gunmen, who were now coming their way at lightning speed. Judas moved his knife swiftly and without hesitation, cutting the throats of the two masked gunmen. The job was done. Now he would have to protect her until he received the call.

Slowly retreating now, Sara recognised this was her best opportunity to escape this madman—a cold-blooded killer, no less. He was not the one to protect her; her dead boyfriend had been wrong about Judas—or maybe even fooled by him. Either way, something told her to get as far away from him as she could. She could feel his internal wounds getting darker by the hour; his lust for revenge was unbearable; his touch and his eyes—his sad sad eyes—were unaware how his twisted but bruised mind was reaching out to her. He was Judas, but she knew he wasn't going to do any more killing today.

Fox News was quick to pick up news of the beach hotel bombing where Sara had stayed. Now it was gone, along with the only person she had loved Black Horse had been her stepfather, and he was now dead, killed inside the hotel he had owned for the last twenty years. Suspects had been held but released without charge. The bomb had gone off in room 111—the room Judas was supposed to be in. The fire had started from his room.

The news on Sara's iPhone was too much for her to bear.

However, Sara's beloved, kind stepfather—the one who had kept her a secret—was not dead.

Things were becoming more and more strange; weirder by the minute. Sara looked at Judas as he drove off in the opposite direction.

'Black Horse died because of me, Sara. Do you hear me?' Judas boomed. 'I don't think you need me to explain why he—'

'I do need you to, but it can wait,' Sara interrupted. 'We are being followed.' She craned her neck in the red Mazda 6 rear-view mirror. Judas slammed his foot down on the gas pedal, the engine screaming, whilst the black Mercedes tailed them with a clear purpose.

'They knew you were supposed to be at the hotel, Judas. They bombed it.'

Judas nodded. 'Yeah, and how did you know I was

staying there? Are you stalking me, Sara? Do you expect me to believe we're both being targeted? And if so. by who? Who, Sara? Answer me! You know who by! Why won't you just tell me what we both know?'

'I don't know what you want me to say. What I do know is if you don't lose those two corporation guys who are looking for us, we'll both be in trouble. It's me they want,' Sara muttered.

'Then let's give them what they want right now!' barked Judas as he roughly pulled up, getting out of the car, leaving the engine running, and pulling out his favourite sniper shotgun. He aimed at the tyres of the speeding Mercedes that was careering towards them. The driver and passenger—two bald guys wearing shades—continued towards Judas, and then suddenly, it pitched up in the sky, tumbled over twice and caught on fire as Judas sent his firing shots on their deadly mission. As the car tumbled, Judas returned to his vehicle where he calmly reached for his ringing phone.

'Are you going to answer that?' Sara shouted. 'It could be the important call we're waiting for!'

'There's no need to shout, babe. All in good time,' Judas responded coolly.

'I am not your babe!' She verified as she positioned the edge of her dagger to his crotch.

Judas looked down and laughed loudly. 'Woman, you are a turn on. I like dangerous, angry women. And I think you like me too!' He smiled at her as he calmly held her hands and slowly removed the dagger. Sara let it go and looked outside the window, nervously rubbing her arms. She could feel visions were soon going to be masking her vision again, and a dark, bruised cloud hung low overhead; the sunny, beautiful day now gone, and she was left alone with what could only be described as a mad soldier—the perfect killing machine.

She couldn't stop focusing on one point, regardless of how dangerous he might be: her stepfather was dead because of him. But then again, it was her fault: she should have left him to die on the highway.

She felt Judas staring strangely at her, and it was then that she noticed blood oozing slowly from his chest. Sara screamed for him to stop, but he was not going to—not unless she got out. She hurried out of the car and ran round to the driver's seat. She demanded he move over. He obeyed as he held his chest in pain whilst laughing uncontrollably at her surprised look. Her tender empathic look was something she tried to hide, but he could see it: this attractive woman was ahead of her time, and there was something hidden and powerful protecting her life. But now he was growing weak, and he had no idea who or what it was.

Judas knew in his heart he did not want to leave her world—not unless she was with him, where he could keep her safe. But he had to wait until his payment was in: killing was all about the money—and always about the revenge.

He turned to look at Sara, who had long tears rolling down her cheeks. 'You don't have to do as they say when they call the killings,' she whispered.

'We'll go to my home, Sara, where you will be

safe,' Judas said. 'We will wait until the heat cools down, then we can make our move—together. You know we would make a great team, you and I. We are cut from the same cloth, Sara Stone.' Judas looked out the window distantly. 'You can slow down now... The cops are not on our tail.'

Sara turned sharply.

'What the fuck was that?' Judas asked as Sara headed in the direction of her own home.

'Shut up and stop your bleeding,' she responded. 'And stop acting like you did not want me to take you home. If I have to die, at least it will be at my home—not yours. Okay?'

'Yeah, I get it. You dig me and I dig you. But you realise neither of us wants to pull the trigger—not yet. I can wait. I've got patience for beautiful women who don't let a man order them around. I think I could get used to you. Weird, right, but you are a strange woman. You make me strange around you...' commented Judas, a look of puzzlement and bewilderment cast over his gaze.

'People judge so quickly, Judas. Trust no one—not even me, at least not until we are safe. Judas, there will be time for you to deal with all of this emotional bullshit, but now you have to get your shit together and start spilling the truth because I will know if you are lying— and you don't want to try to get close to me to finding out,' Sara hissed.

'I've got nothing to hide with. Why did you even bother helping me that day? Along comes Sara, the woman who saves strangers from their fate, but who resents doing it,' Judas said quickly, shooting Sara a glaring look.

'You are lucky I found you,' she said calmly as she looked ahead.

But then, she saw herself covered in blood, a wound to her forehead pouring as she cradled in her arms her two year old child; her baby who had been killed by a kidnapper and left to die. She had not been able to reach her in time to save her. Sara's teary eyes looked out into the distance, and she knew why she was given the gift of seeing through walls killers—like the one sitting next to her. She wished she had a choice, but Judas was a dark soul to bring him back and it was not possible: he would continue to kill and take revenge. He would be a danger to himself and he knew it.

A news update alert beeped on Sarah's iPhone: the Malibu Hotel Inn's owner was missing, and the body they had found was not her stepfather—the native American Black Horse, as he had been known in the town; the Shaman, who people would visit to pay for his visions. He was known across towns and cities for his sermonic trances, where his mind would alter and would pierce though the veil of time to peer into the future. He had been giving permission from his ancestors' gods to see into the future of people and to view their fate. Even in strangers he could see dark secrets. The local police would always visit him to gain insight into a killer on the loose or to find a child who had gone missing or been abducted. Sara had always felt blessed to be a part of his life, briefly before her mother died, but she had inherited the gift. When she was dying, she had told Black Horse to watch over Sara.

Sarah realised she had allowed danger to get too close with her—that not even her stepfather's gifts could save her from her own fate.

Judas's cell was vibrating, but he ignored the call.

'Aren't you going to answer that damn call? What's the matter? You quit your daytime job?' Sara asked sarcastically, a smirk on her face as his eyes turned fiery and angry.

Judas looked at her as though he wished he was somewhere else rather than next to her. He could see why his friend was in love with her and why he had to die to keep her alive—to fight this battle. She did not deserve to be involved in any of this. The corporation would have her on the run. What kind of life was that to live?

Two more business calls needed to be made in person. 'You have to drop me off at this location now,' Judas said, showing Sara an address from a crumbled piece of paper. The scribbles read the address of a local bank, and next to the bank was the local station.

Sara nodded. 'I'm going with you. I'm not letting you out of my sight.'

'Deal,' said Judas playfully.

CHAPTER SIX: CORPORATION

Malibu City Local Sheriff's department

Sara was late for her meeting at the sheriff's office; she had been called in for a special Missing Person's case in the city. The mayor had been reporting missing when he did not show up at home after leaving his office, conveniently next to the police department. He had not been seen now for two days—seemingly gone without a trace. His wife had not received any calls. His mobile phone was switched off and his black Range Rover was also missing. That day, he had told his secretary he was meeting an old friend for lunch: he had gone missing on his birthday: January 12, last seen at 14:11.

It seemed that the major had disappeared without a lead or clue. The police at the local department were baffled, knowing Mayor James Rider was not a man to expected walk away from his home or family.

Sara, however, had notified the department that she was caught up with another case that required her immediate attention, and she would need the file to be sent to her home. Sara's black, aged German Shepherd dog ran out to greet her as she pulled up on her driveway. He playfully wagged his tail, brushing her scarred left cheek, the injury sustained during an attack from an intruder who had followed her home a year before—an escaped kidnapper, no less, who had sought revenge, slashing her face in the darkness. She had responded by shooting him in his gut. She had known that he would be waiting for her—she just did not know when.

She looked at Judas, not understanding why he was staring at her like he was seeing her for the first time. 'Welcome to my humble home,' she said, interrupting his look. 'This is where I usually invite hired killers for dinner,' she said sarcastically.

'Isn't it ironic that a detective specialising in missing people and victims of kidnap would save my life?' Judas asked, edging closer to Sara.

She gently reached out and placed her hands on his now rapidly beating heart. 'Judas.' She pushed him away. She watched as he nervously moved around her home, seemingly with purpose, almost as though he was looking for something. 'Looking for this?' she asked, dangling keys in his face. 'You can have them. But return here, with my car, and don't let anyone follow you here. Have you got it? I know you need to finish the job or they will find us, so do it for your best and only friend—the one you killed.'

'I will do my best to avenge his death,' Judas responded. 'He was a brave solider, but he chose to protect a woman he loved. I know who that woman is, and when I find her, I will make her my prisoner, and then I will kill her—well, if I feel like it,' Judas smirked without humour in his eyes. He glared around Sara's home as though he was being watched.

The surfers were out in full force now. He could see them from the distance, looking down from Sara's home, which afforded a bird's eye view, the house perched at the side of the cliffy hills of Malibu pacific coastal beach. Celebrities—many of whom were also on Judas's hit list, he knew—surrounded the house. His jobs would be easy and the pay-off would be big—and tragic. He smiled at the thought, his mixed feelings for Sara surfacing and wanting to trust her—needing to. The corporation wanted her—they'd said they'd give anything for her—yet he was pulled into the vortex of falling in love with a woman whose boyfriend he killed to save her. The noose was tight and tangled. The damage was already done. And now, Judas knew he had to do the right thing: he must leave now.

As he stood in the doorway of the hall, he watched Sara and considered how easily a woman can forget her surroundings, absorbed by her own thoughts. He marvelled at her perfect body as she slowly entered the shower, glancing over her shoulders to look right at him.

'Oh, I'm sorry... Did you want anything else? Help yourself to a sandwich on the kitchen counter,' she said, clearly unaware of the beauty of her petite body, its shapely legs, her erect nipples. Judas dropped the keys to the floor and unlaced his dirty boots. His bulging crotch was screaming to be released. He tore his bloody shirt away as the button fell to the ground. Bending his knees, he pulled off his pants with lightning speed. He was angry, and wanted to learn to love this woman in another life—but now her body was calling his, and he always swore he'd never leave a damsel in distress.

He slammed Sara's bedroom door shut as his erect,

well-endowed cock took on a mind on its own and guided his every move towards this body of a goddess. Her olive skin, wet now, was all he needed. She screamed as she saw him come towards her.

'No! I won't not let you do this to me!'

He grabbed Sara around the waist and held up her hands above her head, and licked her face like a wolf about to devour its prey—prey wounded by him. As Sara stood like a wounded woman under his spell of manliness, he pushed into her wet, tight, divine, honeycomb, forcing her legs apart as she screamed out his name in pain. He was enormous and he was rough. His thrusting was long and deep, penetrating her sweetness deep within her. She felt the sudden spark of her tangled emotion of passion losing its hold on her mind and body. She opened her mouth to his deep hungry kisses as his gyrating waist held her in motion with his. The fire explored within her quivering loins; she wanted all of him and now. His body, his love... She felt shameless in his arms as he cradled her body, wrapping her legs around his hard backside, her arms supporting her weight against his chest as their racing hearts beat hard against their chests. Their startling passion, their wants and needs met, exploding in their loins, threatening to shatter the safety net of seclusion they had built around their world.

Sara sensed Judas was about to explode inside her if he did not pull out. She was not going to take the risk. She pushed him away, and he allowed her to take charge as she dropped to her knees, massaging his cock in her hands and licking the tip of his enormous dick. He was already coming; she felt his urgency as he lifted her out of the shower and onto the bed. He licked her neck and down to her nipples, before covering every inch of her body. Hungrily, he licked her wet sweetness, her legs trembling either side of his head as he devoured the nectar flowing hotly. She had been waiting for a long time.

He was falling. He did not know why he had allowed this woman—this strange, mysterious creature—to keep breaking his rules, but for now, he didn't care.

He entered her again and grinded inside her slowly and gently, the pair groaning with pleasure and desire. The sensation consumed his senses as she knowingly smiled, sensing his pleasure. It escalated beyond his body. His soul was trapped in his own make-believe world of darkness, and he needed her to save him, to show him the way to the light. He came deep inside of her, calling her name loudly whilst he nibbled playfully on her ear.

He was a skilled lover in bed, and she knew she wanted more of him, as she lay limp in his arms. He kissed her and got up quickly, and walked over to the shower, letting the jets run over his now-tense body. Sara knew she had to let him go now until the time was right, when he would be ready to confess his sins. She knew already she would wait to hear his last words.

As she saw him standing before her now, wet and covered in blood, she saw tears run down his face as he fell slowly into her arms, her dress covered in his blood. 'No!' she screamed out, and ran from the room and into her guest room, breathing hard and choking on sad visions of him. It could and would not happen. She wanted none of this to become a reality. She screamed loudly in her mind as she let go and crumpled to the floor, her knees up to her chin. She rocked back and forth, looking out the window for the magical sunset that was setting. She wanted to be free, just like every sunset. She wanted to see the untouchable. Her life was like that—sunset but without the freedom to love someone. Running away was all she knew, but he was different and dangerous: a killer, responsible for the death of her boyfriend. She knew now, he did it to save her and his family. Judas was his friend but he was also a cold-blooded killer. The memory jolted her back to reality when the door was banged open.

Judas smiled at her wet, naked body as she slowly came across to her and kissed her forehead before unbolting the doors. 'Don't let anyone in if you are not expecting anyone. I promise I will be back and all of this running from that bunch of corrupt government agents will be in the past, and then we can go our separate ways—unless you want to join me on the job,' Judas said in a challenging tone.

Sara stood up, forgetting her nakedness, and ran into the shower. 'Give me a few minutes to get dressed. Let's get them together.'

Judas nodded with a smile. 'Okay. I will have a bite in the kitchen. Hurry up—we've got an hour to get this job done. Malibu Casino will be teaming with life later, and that's where our targets will be hanging. It's going to get very dark in the inner city tonight.' Judas's raised voice travelled throughout the house.

It felt good to Sara having a man in the house who sincerely wanted to protected her, but she knew she needed more than protection from the corporation murderers: she needed to break free from detectives and the crime unit. She remembered she was supposed to be reporting back to them on Judas Ryder—their elusive killer on the run from his hometown. So much was still a mystery to her, but she did not bother asking where he was from. All she had on his file was unknown birth location; he certainly was not from Spain or Texas. She knew they had followed his trail from Utah City to Texas, then back to where she had found him wounded on the side of the road. But now he'd been found, Sara had to know the truth behind his past and what he was doing in this town whilst all hell was breaking loose around them.

She knew had a part in all of this. Her instinct told her to get out of the house now; instead, she hurried out the door and towards the kitchen. She called out to Judas, 'Hey, I am ready. Where are you?'

Silence greeted Sara. There was no sight of Judas in the kitchen. Upon going into the kitchen, Sara found a note left on the counter:

Sara,

I took the Sandwich with me, but I am sorry, my

lovely Sara. I had to lock you in for your own safety. You can't get out—I have all your keys. Don't try because I want to return to find you safe here, where we made love. I think I am already in love with you, but I can't ask you to forgive me for murdering your boyfriend. That's what I do: I kill people. I am hired to kill. I don't ask why... And even if I had left your boyfriend alive, he would have killed you and your stepfather. There is much you don't know about his lies... His letter to you was a lie, Sara. Please, trust me to keep you alive. It's all I ask for now.

Judas

CHAPTER SEVEN: CORRUPT AGENTS

Josh Wes buried his last victim in the desert that evening. She had never made it to the border as he had promised her; she was just another, young, dirty sex worker. No one would miss her or report her missing—and she wasn't alive now to miss her pretty little head, which he'd removed with a swift stroke of a blade.

He drove at break-neck speed. He was in a rush to get out of Mexico City; his memory of his jail term came rushing back. His release from jail after four years had been overdue: he had been sentenced for murders he was assigned by his boss; if he had refused, his three brothers would have been killed. He was only seventeen at the time of the murders. Life did not give him much choice now; all that had changed. Now, he was going to find the border FBI agent who had killed his brothers when he was in jail.

'That son of a fucking bitch has got to know what it feels like…' he shouted aloud. His sweaty palms rubbed anxiously at the steering wheels. His dirty black Ford pick-up truck skidded across the gravel path road, leading to the home of the agent's wife and daughter. He quickly got his rifle shotgun and muttered under his alcohol-laced breath, 'This is for my brothers.' He aimed the gun at the agent's daughter, who was sitting at the kitchen counter, her back to the window. Josh crept up in agent mode towards the garage where the agent's wife's car was parked: she was home. The lights were on, and the midday heat beat down fiercely on his skin. But all too quickly, Sara emerged from behind an oak tree, her silencer aimed at close range, focused upon the notorious killer who was about to take the life of yet another helpless victim of pretty. But not this time: her vision had moved against time.

Joss turned swiftly around and fired shots at Sara, who took covered behind his pick-up truck. She remained hidden long enough to hear his range of shots hitting the truck. She then dived into a nearby bush. She knew what was coming next.

He ran closer to his pick-up, expecting to find her dead behind the vehicle; instead, he found himself facing a barrage of fire as she shot at the gas tank. It exploded in his face, setting him alight in a revengeful stroke of luck.

She walked away unharmed, just as she had witnessed in her out-of-body experience visions of the crime scene. Her very real visions also guided her to the victim's home, and sometimes to the killer. It was always a race to save lives—sometimes to rid the world of killers, one at a time. You just never know where or when killers will strike—or who they are. The victims, however, are always connected in some way.

Sara continued her musings, as her lips slowly snarled at her cursed gift.

The FBI agents who had been on Judas's trail knew who

had lured Josh Wes to his death: it could only be an expert in combat training with knowledge of how to distract a killer in his tracks. When at the scene, the agents uncovered a note secured to the pick-up truck's windscreen, which read *TIME RAN OUT*.

The FBI agent's family were safe.

'I want every lead on Sara Stone. I want all eyes on her from now on: where she sleeps, who she sleeps with, where she eats and, yes, I want her address!' the FBI agent boomed.

'We are not going to find her… She is on the run and she is with someone,' commented a detective from the sheriff's department.

'Detective, is there something you want to tell me that I should know about Sara Stone, or is it that I am going to wait for her to surprise us again? This is not why we hired her! She is crossing the line here!'

'Hold on a minute! You don't know Sara like I do!' stated the detective. 'I know her likes and dislikes. I know where she hangs out. Lately, she has been seen jogging to the beach trail more often than usual—that tells us she is aware of our presence. We can't alarm her now; she will disappear on us. We need her here. She will do as we want, but she needs to feel secure and trusted, and I am the only one she trusts after her boyfriend was killed. She will find out the truth, but you've got to let us deal with this in our way.'

The FBI agent glared.

'I knew her real dad, and she trusts me now. She left me spare keys for her home after she was out on town. She asked me to check in on her dog and take care of him for her. I know her and we're friends.'

Agent Monroe gave him a snarled look of disapproval. 'I will be on your ass if anything goes wrong, do you hear that, Detective? This is not one of your fantasy novels, where you can try and find a way out of the shit you got us into in the first place. You talking about her gift of visions has led us all astray. We didn't buy it then and we still don't now! I know it in my blood she is the one working with all those murderers; she's solving the crimes and then pinning them on others—and if I'm wrong, why didn't she stick around? She is never at any of the crime scenes when she supposedly saves the day! She is hiding *something*, Detective, and something sinister! I could see through her like looking through a glass, and you know something, I think she knows she is going to get caught soon! She is on the run, and she's getting further and further away whilst you lot think she is innocent.'

A teenage girl's cries interrupted the bitter exchange between the agent and the detective.

'Quite clearly, my daughter is traumatised. Do you understand that?' Agent Monroe snarled. 'We need to find Sara, and I *don't* want this get out to the media! My family needs time to recover.'

'Of course,' the detective responded.

'I will need police patrol outside my home until we find her.'

'I'll arrange it. But just one thing: maybe you need to realise that Sara Stone just saved your bloody family mere minutes ago.'

'How dare you, Detective! Get out of my face, man, or you *will* be sorry if you don't!'

'Oh, I'm out of here. By the way, Agent, I've got your back—and I know you've got mine. He got into his car and sped away. He realised now: Sara would need his help. He wanted to help her escape—to get out to Malibu—but she had become a fugitive in her adopted town. Now, only her survival mattered.

The bombs were in place now. Sara knew where and when, but the question was whether she could get there without delays from the agents: they wanted her dead, there was no doubt about them, and time would only be bought if she revealed what she knew about where the payment money was stashed away. The detective knew, it was not the money they wanted but information: knowledge pertaining to the biggest drug dealer; his present location, the time he would arrive to do the deal. They would be taking out the leader of one of the most violent gangs. His training days involved teaching young men how to behead—with practice involving beheading their families. The individuals passing the test would be recruited for his operation—to do his killings, to undertake his biddings. The violence and blood spilt meant his head was worth a lot more than the four million in US dollars buried at the beach-jogging trail. They wanted Sara to find it and bring it to them...

~*~*~*~

Judas nervously shovelled the hole where the cash had been stored in secret. He was working alone, tirelessly and painlessly digging deeper with a shovel. Soon enough, the black garbage bag was showing.

'You can stop digging now.' Sara's presence tugged at his heart. But he was not going to stop—not now. He had to finish the job and get out of this fucking town before it was too late for her—or even him. He needed her to trust him. He had never been one to plead with words—everything was so much easier when equipped with a gun—but he ought to build her trust the way it would normally be done.

'Sara, I need to ask you to trust me.'

'Oh, come on, Judas. You think I'm a fool? Or do you think I'm just your fool because we had sex and I let you into my home? That doesn't mean I will begin to give you any amount of my trust! That's earned, hotshot. I know you want me to be here for you, but I am also someone who is a lot like you—except I don't kill innocent people. I was a victim in the past, and I'm not about to prey on an innocent civilian. I know you killed my boyfriend, Judas. You killed him in cold blood—and all for money. *Money!* And because you wanted to live another day to kill again. So why don't you just drop the shovel and move away from the hole?'

Judas obeyed Sara, and looked directly ahead of her. 'This might not be the best timing, but we've got company.'

Sara turned to look behind.

'It looks like your agent friends are coming. And if we don't move now, they'll kill us and take the money. Trust me, Sara. They're not playing on the same team as you anymore. They don't want you or us anymore. Once they get what they want from you, they will switch your light out, babe.'

Sara's eyes flitted from the agents to Judas and back again.

'Look, I will gladly lay my life down for a smart woman, but not a stupid one. And if you get us caught, you're one of the stupid ones.'

Whilst she was distracted, Judas managed to throw her over his broad shoulders. He began to run with her down the beach. Sara did not protest; she knew at that moment that he was right. He was saving them both from the agents she once thought she could have trusted with her life. And now they knew her address: they would find her.

Judas threw Sara into the passenger seat and took control of the driver side. The truck sped away, leaving the agents gathering the black bag of money.

Judas waited a short while before staking out the agents. He waited for them to leave, before following them to their hide out.

'Why are we following them?' Sara asked, perplexed. 'It is too risky. We have to find the other bomb and we have to find my stepdad. He wasn't at the hotel.'

'How do you know he wasn't there?'

'He sent me a text saying he was safe, but that he

did not want me to find him now. He said it was too dangerous and he needed time. He said to find the ones responsible for bombing the hotel, and that he wanted me to leave.' Sara's eyes glistened with tears. 'He thinks it's time I move out of Malibu. Maybe he's right. Maybe it is time…'

CHAPTER EIGHT: UNDERGROUND WARS

'Where would you go, Sara?' Judas asked curiously whilst driving towards the sunset. Its amber glow was breath-taking, creating halos across the Malibu coastline.

'Anywhere. Somewhere new where I can't get into trouble.'

Judas felt comfortable with this remarkably strange, clumsy woman, who didn't seem to know how to keep from falling for dangerous men like him. 'Look at me, Sara.'

Sara looked at Judas, caution in her eyes.

'You are in love with me, aren't you?' His heart was racing

'We are about to be taken out by a bunch of corrupt undercover agents and you're going to ask me something like that? But to answer your stupid question, I would not fall for you even if you were the last man on the planet. Your mind is twisted, Judas. I am not gullible like those women you usually find yourself in bed with.'

Sara had to keep reminding herself that all he was to her was a killer, and the worlds they lived in were so different.

'You set me on fire,' Judas said, laughing out loud, mockingly. 'On the upside, at least you know how to tell a lie to your bruised mind, but your body contradicts you,' he said, shamelessly laughing out loud at his own thoughts. 'You keep so much inside.'

Deep down, Sara was fearful of losing him, and the

fear of knowing he was not completely human—he lacked empathy, compassion and, seemingly, any true emotion. He was not the kind of man she should be involved with. He was only concerned about finishing his own bloody killings.

'I need coffee,' Sara said, desperate to change the subject.

Judas pulled over when he spotted a coffee shop. He switched off the engine and got out. Sara was already out of the truck, running off in the other direction, away and across the road to a nearby hotel, where she was supposed to have a room booked. She suddenly stopped, feeling Judas nearby, running like a madman. He caught up with her, breathless, and slapped her hard. She fell against the wall, blood running down from her face, and then suddenly everything went black.

She heard his voice screaming her name, pleading with her to wake up. She could feel his warm grasping breath on her face as he held onto her, and he sobbed in her arms, the noise fading.

Agent Monroe was searching the detective's home whilst he was tied to a chair in his living room. His breathing was ragged. The agent hurled a number of threats to the helpless detective; all he could do was sit and take them.

Through the French doors leading to the patio and the backyard, there was a group of agents discussing, in a low tone, the fate to await the detective. He knew it was time for him to die; his secrets of Sara would die with him. He was not a crooked cop—he did this privately to stay away from men like Agent Monroe. He would now have to rethink his make-up story and give them proof of how to find her and where she was heading. They would have to do as he said.

Malibu had some rough weather coming tonight, and the detective wanted to distract them with the news of the storm to delay their search of Sara. He knew she was safe with the one man that could and would protect her.

Sara awoke with a headache. She put her hand to her head to find a cut, and realised she was in the emergency room. A nurse appeared. 'Oh, you are awake. Good,' she said in an Irish accent.

'Who brought me here?' Sara asked.

Attending to her cut, the nurse stopped what she was doing. 'Well, the attendant told us the man who brought you in was also wounded; he had a gunshot wound. He is in the operation theatre right now. It may take a whilst to remove the bullet; it is lodged between his shoulder blades.'

Sara blinked, trying to absorb the news. 'Is he alright?'

'He is a little messed up, but he asked us to make sure you don't leave without him. Of course, you may do as you please. To be honest, I think he feels he is superman, trying to save you when he needs saving himself.' The nurse smiled. 'So, is he your man? He certainly seems to have a soft spot for you. He seemed very concerned.'

'No.' Sara shook her head. 'And please, I can't see him again. Please keep him away from me. He did this to me.' She pointed to her head.

'Okay. Just stay calm. You can always make a report. For now, concentrate on relaxing.' The nurse left the room.

Sara wanted to fall asleep and wake up next to her dog. She wrenched in pain as she tried to move. She wanted to get out of there as soon as she could; she wanted the day to end. She wobbled and tried to balance herself. She steadied herself on the chair next to the bed, discomfort and pain surging through her body. She looked out of the window, waiting for the right time to escape. But all too soon, a deep trance-like state came over her, and as though she was falling into a sleep, she let go. She entered the realm of her visions where events unfolded like a 3D movie.

The hospital reminded her of the smell of death. The room was cold and dark unforgiving. Doctors and nurses were working, peering over an unconscious familiar man; she knew him too well by now. His chest was being worked on, and there was a bloody mess where a bullet had penetrated the skin. The doctors worked quietly, or maybe she could not hear what they were saying. A halo glowed around the man's head, but it was fading. The doctors left the room, and it was then that she suddenly heard her name whispered, softly at first. It was Judas: he was standing next to her, smiling, shirtless, his wounds open, close to his heart.

'You don't know who I am and what I can do to save you. I know who you are, Sara, and I will find you wherever you go.' His image began to fade away.

Sara looked around the hall but could see nobody. She looked around the operation room, and saw the man taken out by some nurses, followed by two agents in black suits. He was wheeled out of the theatre, and she could feel the sense of danger. She had to get to him now or he would be dead.

She closed her eyes and raced back to her room where she thought she was dreaming, intent on waking herself, but her tired body was fast asleep.

She suddenly felt a sharp spasm and was met with the sensation of falling though air. She woke up and quickly tried to move, but she found she was tied to a chair. She realised she was no longer in hospital, but was back home in her house and there, next to her, Judas was lay on the bed on which they made love.

Her hands were tied behind her back. The chair was the antique chair she had bought at an auction in Paris whilst on a job. Her passion for antiques, such as her rare antique book collection where she kept her collection of daggers from Turkey, was an original piece from the ancient temples of the Arab princes of the past. Now, however, the bookcase was a heap of broken glass and wood. Her rare books had been torn apart and were now lay between the cover of the rarest book from her collection. The daggers were under the chair where the book had been flung in haste.

The agents quietly discussed what to do with her and Judas. The door was slightly ajar, and she craned her neck to see how many of them they were facing. There were two Asian women, maybe in their twenties, who were clearly operatives working undercover. She had met them in China when working on the last case. They had assisted her with finding two missing teenagers from the US, whose father was a Film Director in LA. When his children had gone missing, he had called Sara for help. Their only lead was the Convention of Arts.

The teenagers' father had done a documentary on air pollution in Shanghai, which was set to become a film, *China Stardust*. It had been kicking up a storm in the US, and its trailer had gone viral across Japan and Europe. The backlash had involved his sons being stolen, forcing their hands to remove the movie from the radar grid before it hit the big screen; however, it had been released regardless—unbeknownst to the studio.

Mr Jing Min had been in partnership; he did not give permission, but the pressure to release was strong. If they did not release it, he'd known, it would have been stopped.

The story centred on two warring gangs' families, stemming back to the days of the Chinese Dynasty and its emperors, spanning to modern times. Various government agents were detailed as being responsible for killing present-day members of the family who had lived in America, as well as those that had lived in small villages. Their land had been taken from them to build skyscrapers; the water was contaminated.

All of this was detailed in a file stored by Sara, which had been stolen from her house three weeks before. The intruder had taken the file; there had been no forced entry. The door had to have been opened by her friend, the detective, who had worked on numerous cases. He had to be the culprit.

CHAPTER NINE: CHINA'S SECRETS

Murky evening skies, foul smelly cabs, breath, and her dear friend, Detective James...

His hands covered his mouth and nostrils. He felt dizzy with the foul smell. 'Has something crawled up in here and died?' he asked with a laugh.

'Smog from the air,' the driver said, smiling and seemingly embracing the smog filling the cab. The city highways of Shanghai were filled.

He was never going to leave Sara.

For four days Sara did not get the code call from her contacts. She knew something was strange. But she wondered what could realistically be done. Her visions were clear enough, but getting access to the checkpoint was the difficult part. So far, she did not have a plan in place—unless her undercover agent for the US, Agent Melina, a descendant of royalty, called.

'Let's return to the hotel,' she decided. 'I sense she'll be more likely to meet us there than take us back to the hotel.'

'Okay. Back to the hotel,' said the driver, smiling at Detective James.

The cab travelled past a group of aged women, all with brooms, who were sweeping the sidewalks, keeping them active and clearly their minds away from the poverty they had to endure. They humbly and quietly worked in groups, spread out throughout the city and amongst the skyscrapers. The street's dust was visible;

the grey smog looked like a deep fog, hanging in the air, engulfing the city streets. The people were saturated; they could not escape it once they were in the street. The countryside was free from the pollution, but the dust was blowing in from the Mongolia Desert, creeping upon the millions throughout the night.

The area was cold and damp, and the frequent earthquakes in recent years had destroyed buildings. The bird nest stadium was a sight for sore eyes; it was a genius feat of china.

Sara knew she had to find the teenagers quickly before it was too late, but it was no use: she could not pick up any threat to her. As always, Sara was given untouchable cases. But whenever she was losing faith, she would say to herself, 'Don't let your heart give you a reason to hate. When you give your life to someone or something, stand by it. Die with it. But don't let it go'. Those words were spoken from Sara's heart; she needed to see, to know, why this was happening and how she could save Judas, whose life meant more to her right now than the lives of the agents who had invaded her life and shattered her privacy.

Reality only brings anger and suspicion of the people you have to work with.

A messenger walked into the hotel lobby. The guests awaiting transport were screaming and running into the lobby. Sara eyed a black sports bag at the corner of the fountain in the middle of the lobby. She knew the bomb would go off in five minutes. She bolted out of the door with the detective; she told him a bomb was in the bag next to the fountain. Detective James moved with speed, running run towards the fountain and picking up the bag gently. He walked out at a hurried pace, taking the bag across the street and running towards the bridge, He flung the bag into the river flowing beneath the bridge. The bag sailed down the river rapidly, and quickly sunk below the surface. It exploded at exactly 11:05 am.

Sara had been held for a long time in the cell at the city jail. Detective James was also in a cell and was demanding to be released. Sara told them she was working with the CIA agent from Russia, and it was as if she had uttered magic words for them to set free the teenagers. They took her into the next room, where the teenagers were being held. They were scared and shaken up, but alive. Sara knew they would have to release them to her; they had no choice.

The undercover agent was working together with the state to release the teenagers as they promised, and signed an agreement for the film not to be shown in their country cinemas. This was their way of keeping the peace in their country, protecting them from any sort of people outside their realm of illusions who fled their villages, choosing to live in America and Europe. However, when the news had broken about the kidnapping, the film had gone viral; Sara had no control over the leak. They would never forgive her and they had been waiting for this day.

Judas was their bait, but she was not going to give them something even more important.

They were stealing the water from the springs and selling off the land to foreign businesses, such as the one Judas had been working for. He did not care about the lives of people—especially the ones on the list. He was void of human emotions; his heart was frozen, but she wished it was not. Tears ran down her face as she pleaded in her heart.

She was hit across the face by one of the Chinese agents. 'You remember now, don't you? The shame you brought to my country. You and your boyfriend killer here will know what it is to betray a great nation like my country. We work hard to discipline our people. You work hard at breaking that system.' Sara was slapped again, sending her head reeling. Her face was bruised now.

'Yes, Min, I remember you, but can we do this in private? Close the door to my bedroom and I will let you do to me what you want. I know nobody is leaving my house until they find what they came for, and I am the only one that knows him. You studied his profile, didn't you, Agent Min?'

The agent narrowed her eyes, puzzled by her lack of information on Judas.

'Judas has the map to where the file is located, but it's stored in his head. You don't want to mess with his head. He suffers from PSTD and he can become very violent very quickly. It takes nothing to trigger his frequent outbreaks. He is a cold-blooded killer. He values nothing because he has no family, no ties. His memories evade him. His traumatic memory keeps replaying his tragic experiences in war, and the powerful men who drag his soul kicking and screaming into the dark waters of hell where he was taught to kill without thinking. He carries out revenge killings, working for the same company that is draining your springs and rivers. Soon they will stop running into the cities; its supply will be cut off. The new China will have exactly what it wants: a dusty, thirsty environment where natural resources don't come cheap, where millions will live without water. This won't solve your country's water woes or your country's thirst; it will only be on the black list that will appear very soon. Your country will be at war, and millions will die from contaminated water through deliberate poisoning. Your government is killing your people slowly, and it doesn't even bother you.'

'Why should it?' the agent asked mockingly.

'I know you were born there... The spring is on your father's land—well, it was before they killed him. Or did someone convince you it was an accident? I was there. I saw them kill your father because he tried to protect his land. They are using you to shut up the people that could help you and your people. If they don't work for them, well, you know better than me what their Fate will be.'

'I don't believe a word you say. You are lying. My

father shot himself. He committed suicide when my mother left him. You tell lies about my country. The people of China help their citizens to be better in life, and they provide jobs and homes for them. Your lies are meaningless. *You* are the traitor, the betrayer. *You* will die for what you have unleashed, but first the file… Tell me where it is and I will consider letting you go. But if you don't, I will kill you here.'

'You can kill me, but Judas has the file in his head, so kill him and the file will be lost forever. But I can get him to tell me where it is. So maybe you should spare us. By the way, did you read my profile about my gift of sight? I can see where he has it… This way, we all get what we want.' Sara watched the agent, determination in her eyes. 'Agent Min, let me help you.'

Agent Min was affected by Sara's hypnotic voice as she silently untied Sara. She gazed into Sara eyes and then glanced nervously towards the door. 'I will give you thirty minutes with him alone here, but no more.' Agent Min shrugged and left the room, locking the door on her way out.

Sara grabbed the knife from the fallen books. She acknowledged that her life was hanging by a thread, and she could not trust anybody—not even Judas. He was the key to all that was happening; he was a curse and bad omen. He was in her life but, despite everything, she did not want to lose him. Her thoughts shamed her; she was betraying herself, and he was damned with a sentence to hell. But that had nothing to do with now: she needed his help to escape.

'Sara…' he groaned. 'I need you.'

'Shut up,' she spat. Even now, her brown eyes furiously trained on Judas. She was an intelligent woman, but she was confused, dazed, angry and afraid.

He had allowed this woman to enter his mind and his heart in this pivotal tide of an unforgiving and tangled web. He allowed his company to create lies around his existence. Judas felt dizzy but alive; she made him feel strong. He knew the danger they were facing in the next room, and so he knew he needed to put his plans in place. 'Tell me that Asian chick bitch did not hurt you…' Judas was in a rage. He wanted to rip out the agent's throat with his hands for daring to hurt Sara. She felt a strong urge to protect her, and it shocked his body like a thunderbolt. The pain would come after, he acknowledged, as soon as she found out why he had killed her solider boyfriend. He knew she deserved to know; she was an intelligent, sophisticated woman. He needed to prove his worth, and he realised he loved her with all his heart. It would even haunt him even beyond death. Sara's home had been invaded, and now he had to stop the madness. 'Sara, listen. I swear I will make this bad dream go away. They will pay. They are the ones corrupting the system in silence. Their fronts are always the soldiers who give their lives and reputations to protect their ways of corruption and greed. They add fuel to the fire, keeping the country warring forever. It benefits the masses of their elite forces.' He was cracking, and he knew home was coming closer. He felt the tugging of the magnetic pull. 'The world needs to know.' His deep, throaty voice softened gently. 'I could help you escape, but I have to convince them I am still in charge of this operation. What sort of weapon do you keep in this room?'

Sara looked at him and slapped him hard, pointing the knife to his face. 'You see this knife? It has been stained with the blood of ancient Sumerians, and I don't want to use it on you, but you are the one they want—not me.'

'Hold on... won't you listen to me? I have a plan to get us out of this. And then you can run as far away from me as you want when this is all over. But if you want me to, I will look for you. And I think you will. You could not resist me from the first time you took me home, like a wounded stray dog at the side of the road. I am irrespirable from you.'

Sara raised her hand and aimed for his face, planning on cutting him. She raged on the inside. Judas grabbed her with one hand and kissed her forehead, trailing his tongue over her bruised face. Sara melted in his arms; she wished it was another time and place; she wished she was just like one of his other women. This would be less painful.

'Give me the knife.' He gently removed it from her grasp. Quickly, he cut her arms with the blade before muffling her scream beneath his meaty hands. She struggled to escape, but he held her as he cut her hands. 'Do that one more time, and I will kill you right here!' Judas screamed, alerting the agents.

The Asian opened the door cautiously, looking

around and saw Sara struggling in his arms, her bleeding arms catching her attention. The other agents rushed into the room. Judas jumped into action, letting go of Sara and pushing her to the floor.

The agent took her gun and effortlessly sprayed bullets. Judas knew he had to help Sara escape; it didn't matter what happened to him. The agents fell quickly as, suddenly, Black Horse appeared, spraying his high-powered rifle, taking three agents out.

'Judas, you must leave now. I will clean up this mess. It works well but you can have your piece back.' He handed the rifle to Judas.

'Where is Sara?' Judas asked, searching around.

'I arranged for a cab to take her to the airport. She must leave now. They will be after her. In case you haven't noticed, the heat will be here any minute—I will take them for you. But let her go. Now you go off to Canyon Trail Park. Take care of her; make sure she reaches her destination. She is like my own blood—she is my daughter. Now go.'

Judas did as he was told. 'Thanks, man. I will make it up to you someday soon, I promise.' With that, Judas left, heading towards the woman he needed, his heart beating warmly.

Judas knew he did not want to return to the abyss of the torture chamber he called a job. There had to be no turning back now. Sara was why he still existed in this dark, broken world he had created. He realised his mother, a mental case, and his father, a violent drunk, were to blame for his high school dropout. His dad would beat him and spit on him for being a weak boy, and so he had taught himself the art of survival in a cruel world where nobody—not even your own blood—could be trusted.

His bags were in the truck. He returned to get them, although recognising the risk. He crept behind the truck, and saw the cops coming in from the side. They were on Sara's porch, and it was then that he saw Black Horse come out of the house, Sara as his hostage. He handed her over to the cops. Sergeant Rick Ashley took her roughly by the arms and pushed her up against the deputy car. They handed her over to the deputy and his agents, who had arrived on the scene. Roughly, they covered Sara's head with a black hood, and took her to a heavy tainted sub. They sped off quickly.

Judas acted quickly, his head spinning. He did not want any harm to come to her, but he had to know what Black Horse was planning. He knew now: they had trusted someone who didn't deserve it. Sara would be handed over to her enemies, saving Black Horse's ass and lying about Sara. That didn't sound like the man Sara had come trusted her whole life.

'Make one bad move and I will blow this place to pieces.' Judas held up a grenade, his index finger clinging to the pin. 'Make that fucking call now!'

'She is fucking dead anyway… It is her or us,' screamed Peter.

'I don't bluff. You know the game is almost over. This is not Iraq. We are not fighting a foreign country. Listen, I don't know why you are mixed up in this shit, but just don't do anything stupid. We can fight this together. Trust me, Judas.'

'No, I don't trust you, but thanks for the offer,' Judas replied, dialling into his iPhone.

Judas gave the phone to Peter.

'Return Sara back here now. No, don't ask questions. Return her.' Peter gave Judas a smirk as he disconnected the call. 'Now what, Rambo? You got what you want. So where do we go from here? You shoot us cops now? You put the phone in the fish tank next to you? You know you aren't going to make it far from here. We will be on your tail.' Peter tried hard to distract Judas, to instil fear and make him nervous, but deep down, Peter knew Judas was not going to budge: he had worked with him side by side on minefields. He knew he was skilled and talented. His gifts were much the same as Sara's: he could sense danger close by, even when no one else could see it. His ability was a secret the navy kept closely guarded. 'Judas you will be on the run and hunted down.'

Judas squeezed the trigger and fired five rounds of ammunition, killing them all. Their lifeless bodies fell backwards; they had no time to return fire. The element of surprise always worked. He walked over to Peter, who was now gasping for breath, blood running down his face. His eyes were finally accepting his fate. He stared desperately as Judas towered over him.

'You forget I am a hunted man,' Judas whispered. 'I chose this way of life. I look to rid the world of scum like you.'

The sound of a vehicle approaching stopped Judas from continuing. They pulled up, and Sara walked over without the hood over her head. Judas recognised the driver had left the engine running and was on the lookout. Judas aimed his sniper gun at the bonnet when Sara kicked the agent in the crotch and watched as they crumbled in pain. Judas quickly fired at the vehicle and grabbed Sara. They ran quickly, jumping into the truck. Judas pushed his foot down firmly on the gas pedal, slamming the door as Sara yelled.

The explosion blew the two agents high into the air above them. The sky was engulfed with thick black smoke. Sirens screamed and rushed.

When passing through the smoke and chaos, Sara sat in shocked silence. She needed an explanation for Black Horse; she could not believe her own stepfather— the man who had raised her—had so heartlessly given her up to killers.

'I think Black Horse knew how it was all going to end, you know,' Judas told her.

'He had openly communicated with me ever since I discovered how to use my special gift. He always guided my mind, told me it was alright to have this power, that the gods would guide me—especially the spirit of the wolf. He said he knew something about all of this before it happened.'

Judas looked at her and shook his head.

'Maybe he was trying to tell me this was the only way out for him and us.'

'When he spoke his last words to me, I could see in his eyes he wanted me to kill him. I did not—he is still alive in there.'

'You spared him after all he did. Maybe now you can start to give yourself a break every once in a while.'

'I want to keep surprising you—in a good way.' Judas looked into her eyes—those eyes were bright, able to drown a man in their power. He felt hungry around her and needful of her love. His thirsty heart longed to drink in her beauty. If only he had time. If only his assignment was not a picture of her. If only he could make up for the betrayal, the lies and the darkness—all threatening to engulf his need for her.

He was finally home. She was home.

CHAPTER TEN: ESCAPE

Judas was in increasing pain; the headaches were coming in flashes. He was awake now and braced himself for the rippling searing pain that threatened to weaken and slow down his pace of escape. He was about to pull out his knife—a shining blade hidden in his boots—when he felt a hand squeeze his shoulder blades. He bit down on his bottom lips to endure the excruciating pain. 'Where do you think you are going?' Agent Monroe asked. Two border agents looked on glaringly.

Sara was out cold; she was tied to the chair, her head drooped. They had clearly drugged her.

'What the fuck did you do her?' Judas raged.

'Oh, you mean your girlfriend here? When did you start caring for your assignments, Judas?' Agent Monroe asked, with deadly intent in his voice. Monroe was responsible for cleaning up the operation.

'Are you and your two agents all they have now?' Judas asked. 'You are the clean-up crew. Yeah… If you don't let her go, none of us will leave here alive. There is a bomb under this bed, and it has five minutes to go. And guess what? Only I can stop it!'

'Really?' asked Monroe, unfazed. 'You've still got game, Judas, and here I was thinking you had softened up. Why don't you get your ass under there and diffuse it for us, eh? It is part of your special training. On the other hand, you can leave it there and let it blow us up, just like you blew up a family of women and kids in Iraq by mistake. Do you remember that? Yeah, of course you do. You sure know how to mess up big time, don't you? Even now, you are still good at it.' Agent Monroe sneered at Judas.

Judas moved like a cobra, easing his way closer to Agent Monroe's gun. He swiftly wrapped his hands around his neck, putting Monroe in a dead lock and firing the gun in the agent's hand with key precision. The two surprised agents fell, stumbling as bullets rippled through their bodies. Judas turned the gun back on the agent, forcing Monroe to shoot himself in his throat. He fell backwards, holding his neck as blood flooded through his fingers.

Judas hurried to free Sara, who was drowsy but becoming more alert. As he untied her, she took her dagger away from her draw. The file was gone, but the sub clip was safely between the books—right where she had hidden it on her bookshelves. 'Let's go. We've got to get out.'

'No,' protested Sara, 'not until you tell me where you are taking me.' Sara pulled away and walked towards her car, still unsteady on her feet.

'Okay, fine. I am going somewhere where we can't be traced. We need to stay below the radar for a few days until we can decide who is behind the hit killings— not that I care, but it seems to mean a lot to you and I don't think you want me to let you out my sight. Get in my van or I will leave you here when the cops come— which they will. You don't want to be here.'

Sara responded with an icy glare.

'I am sorry but things are bad as they are, but I have no control over this situation. It seems even my best friend Black Horse, your stepdad, is caught up somehow in all of this. He has disappeared, just like the other agents. The file is what they are after, and I know things are going get uglier by the minute. Please, Sara, trust me for once and I will protect you.'

'I will go with you, but only because you've the file—I saw you take it,' she spat at Judas.

Judas laughed. 'Maybe you saw that in your blurred visions—quite clearly, they're not always accurate! But, Sara, we can fight all you want when we get to the hidden hill. Now, however, is not the time!'

Sara finally got into the truck, and they drove in silence, passing the vegetable beds, fields and vineyards. Sara looked on at the beauty, pondering a normal, quiet life; home and rose gardens. But fate was a cruel joker, and she knew she would never live the ideal life.

Police sirens screamed, and vehicles flew past them on Highway Route 1. Now, they were the hunted.

'Judas, can you go any faster?' Sara asked frantically.

Judas shouted angrily, scolding her. 'Calm down! We have to drive at a normal speed or we will attract unwanted attention. Judas was stern and harsh with Sara because he wanted her to see him as the only man who she could trust. 'You need to trust me.'

'How can I trust you? You've proven to me I can't trust you, so where do we go from here?'

'Sara, I am allowing you to see my hideout.

'You mean your man-cave?' Sara interrupted teasingly.

Judas's patience was running thin. 'Yes. I mean no! It's just where I live for now. Nobody else has seen this place.' Judas looked at her empathically. He needed to hear and feel her emotional response.

He was as gifted as she was; it was the reason the military had held an interest in him. They trained him to kill without a conscious for people; he was like a hybrid, separating himself slowly and painfully from empathy and compassion.

'Sara, just fly with me. We've got to stay together.'

Her soulful eyes searched his. She should have been scared, but strangely she was not. He was an intimidating man with his bulk of muscle and scars, but she didn't appear afraid of him. Her hands slipped to his chest, her fingers splayed wide. She drew in her breath as if she felt the same burning in her lungs. 'Judas, I am trying so hard to save you, but I don't think it can happen—even though we both want it to. Her tearful eyes showed her honesty, her love, her shame for loving him.

He bent his head and kissed her fingers. He kept his eyes on the road ahead, leading to his villa. 'I need saving,' he said, finally choosing to give her the raw truth, 'but sending me away won't accomplish that. Fight for us. That's all I ask. You know me: we are not like other people. Maybe our gifts are responsible, but you know me, Sara. I know we barely know each other, but how can I tell you things I've never told anyone else?

Your body responds to my mine. Your mind is fighting, but your heart and soul know I'm the one for you. So please, just give us a chance.'

She sighed and smiled. 'I hope you know the police can find us. I hope you have thought of an escape plan.'

'Sara, you know they are not coming here. Look at me.'

Her eyes blinked, glazed. She finally saw in his eyes the raw trust he was willing to give her.

'Judas, guarding yourself keeps you safe when you are hunted.' She thought about her work: she was not supposed to get this close to the killers. But then she wondered: was Judas more than a killer? He was a lost soul, searching for redemption in her. She was scared for this strange, cold, deceptive man. He did not open up easily. And his boss was yet to be revealed to her.

As they drove up a pathway, the view was unbelievable; it was so secluded—even an army of men could be locked away. The coastal city bay could be seen with a bird's eye; the sloping vineyard was an added bonus to the estate. It possessed magical beauty, and was the perfect place to stay out of trouble or too bunker down off the radar.

When they were out of the car, Sara decided to check out the place. Under a shaded sycamore tree was a man, hanging. Sara looked at him, but when she looked back he was standing under the tree, calling her. He looked like a Mexican labourer, but he slowly faded away. She pointed to him, speechless, but Judas saw nobody there.

'It's just us, my princess. There are only ever workmen in the vineyard. They won't bother us. We have this whole old rustic home to ourselves—unless you want to try and run away from me. I will allow you to leave at any point if you can find your way back. There is no phone reception here; no emails, no computers. But there are lots of candles, and there are outdoor grills to do our cooking—something I am good at. I've always wanted to retire here with the right woman; someone who can tangle her web tightly around me—tight enough for me to want the simply, uncomplicated life. But that will be in another lifetime. For now, let's not allow the house to get any colder.' He stared into her eyes with a longing to hold her, yet he did not he want to: he needed to be sure she needed to hold him, and she was not making any suggestion that implied she wanted his arms around her.

Judas knew she was fighting her feelings for him and, in some way, which made him happy. Men like Judas weren't a common breed: they don't nest anywhere for long; their home is on the road, living like a caveman, surviving on a day-to-day basis. Hit men still practice not staying in one place for too long; it becomes more like an addiction, moving and relocating as soon as the heat is close. The hit men sense fear; they know when they are being hunted in their sleep, and in their waking hours their life is hunted by their own fear of death—ever close—yet living another day allows accumulating wealth to travel and indulge in sinful luxuries. The world is the oyster of hit men: they are able to roam, to taste, to take, to plunder and to kill. It is a living, and this dying breed does it for a living—one way or another, whether legally or illegally. And they recognise that the ultimate standoff can be their last.

Judas kept his eyes on the clock; the minutes were counting down his last seconds with Sara. He could not believe everything was about to change—within the next twelve hours. If only he could go back to the past and kill the people that had held him against his will. They had chosen this destiny for him; he did not belong to himself, not since the day he had found out about his gift of predicting when the next terror plot would be hatched. He could see though his targets' twisted, deadly minds. He could predict the next move, but he could not see any of this without being in the same location. He needed proximity. And now he had grown tired of being used for his gift.

He cursed the day he found out how to use his talent. He cursed the fact he had trusted the orphanage chapel priest with his secret. He had been betrayed, and so he would never again trust anyone. And then, so long after all of this, he had received his most recent assignment, detailing his last job, located at the horizon high, up in the vineyard valley.

Jolted back to reality, Judas recognised he had someone he cared enough for to protect. The realisation made his hair stand up on end in fear of how close she was. He was a killer who was reluctant to kill again— and all because of her. Every cop in the city would be on his or her trail; time would be the only protector now. He watched Sara breathe in with a smile on her face, almost as though she was breathing in the villa's old rustic history. Guilt overcame him: she could have left him to die in the ditch where she had found him, and now she has to pretend to hate him enough to get the job done.

He had come to learn what it is to be truly at ease with another human being. He cursed the fact that he had been made into this pitiful human being, but nothing could change that. It was too late. Sara was now in his life, but it felt like lies were caging him like a wild beast. He wanted answers. But he wished he had not fallen this unforgiving but sensual and mysterious woman who did not understand who she was in this broken world yet who saves lives thousands of miles away from her real home.

Judas quietly hugged Sara—the space in her arms was all they had. She was lost in the beauty of the vineyard. 'Are you hungry?' He wrapped his arms around her gently, painting her neck with delicate kisses.

Sara wanted this moment to last for the rest of her life. She kept reminding herself that darkness was creeping its way forward, threatening their corner of the world where nothing was what it seemed and where lies kept them apart and together. How could she tell him now? It was too late.

His caresses overwhelmed her senses. She felt his love and his hate for loving her; she could feel his regrets that he was no longer a man but a beast. She could feel his silent rage—his almost hopeless weakness for her. She knew his love for her was real; his eyes told her things she'd rather not know. She knew of the pain and the killings. She knew he craved the indulgence of his next kill; she could sense that it kept him living his current life, maintaining the existence he chose, surrounding him with this unforgiveable yet fulfilling darkness. His soul was already black; the light was fighting its way back in. Sara held on to him tightly. She wanted to bring him back to the light, but he was too proud to control his own fears of letting go of his companion of darkness.

'Where do we go from here? Judas, I can't go back to my home It is gone,' Sara said gently.

'Maybe you should return to your real hometown, Sara... Where your parents lived,' Judas suggested.

'When were you going to admit to me that you know all there is to know about me? Did you know I had to run away from my London home because of my identity? Did you know I had to change my name the day I left? Did you know I was supposed to return to Iran with my parents? I kept all of this truth to myself—not even the agents who are after me know who I am or know my country of origin. All information about me was destroyed with my birth files.'

Judas listened patiently.

'I was Sara Stone. I did not know who I was in this world or even why I was chosen to do this work for the government. I had no choice but to write about my work as an undercover detective—until I found traces of their link to murders and deaths, trafficking and kidnapping. It was all part of the network of lies fuelling the intense hate for my country and myself. I would never return to Iran because my soul, Judas, will remain in my hometown of London. Behind the church, in a quaint two-bedroom apartment, where the white chapel with the pigeon-stained Virgin Mary... That is my home.'

Judas stroked at Sara's cheek.

'You know what I am talking about,' she said, glaring at him whilst her tears revealed her true emotion.

He playfully licked the salty tears from her beautiful face. She pulled away but he held on, making himself feel it was time to return to his world and time with her—but not yet. He could not take her there yet; they both had to finish the job in this time and at this place in this world. All of this was home to them both, albeit in a different time.

As they gazed deeply into each other's soul, all they wanted to know was revealed to them: no words could take their place. Words were known to deceive humans; all people were deceived by their thoughts and confused by their words; neither was a real way of expressing—at least for those that travel through time to fight a cause, even if they exist as lovers in a world to which they both belong. But somehow, they would find their way out. They had to face what was coming—and it was coming fast.

'We need to go inside and await our unwelcome guests.' Judas tilted her head gently and planted a tender but passionate on his woman—his Sara. He tasted her sweet lips, sealing his trust and giving her his heart throughout time.

The wind was picking in the distance. Judas could see the silent visible bluish wormhole tear in space and time from a distance. It was getting closer, and when it arrived, they would have only 48 hours to enter.

Judas knew Sara had come here willingly, on a mission, to try and stop him. But he had to end her mission here, in this place. The Chinese agents were everywhere, and the water mafia corporation was on their trail. The red water death file would never be taken seriously the war between the villagers and the Chinese agency would not stop: the red death was real, and the water of the springs was killing the people in the village. They could not sell it; after all, all who consumed it died after the young chemist was forced to use poisonous chemical that killed instantly. One cup of the water was as lethal as nerve gas, and it affected a whole community. Now, it was too late: millions were dying. There was no preventive cure—at least not yet.

The bodies of the dead were thrown in ditches and burnt to ashes, which were scattered by the winds into the springs. The souls haunted the springs, diving like restless spirits. The agents were ordered to kill their parents; the government agencies thought they were not fit to live in modern times of change. Accordingly, they were trained to obey any orders for their countries—a requirement that would need to come first, above all things in their life. Now, if Judas was to take her with him, back into his world, what would it look like? Dying here was all an illusion; the body and soul live on in another dimension. Mirroring worlds to Earth did not exist in other worlds like this one: no one walked into a room late for a meeting or a date; it was different. His memory did not allow him to remember much then; in this world, he was about to break the rules of nature—*his* nature. He would need to embrace the one thing he could not leave behind in this dark, cruel world: she was the one he came for, she was the one he needed to take with him into his world. She would leave with him unless they were both killed. The future looked dim; their choices would end tonight before the morning light hit the horizon of this world. And if they did not make the right choice, they would have to remain until the wormhole returned when the planets were next aligned. They would not age until then. He hoped Sara could remember where she really came from: another Earth like this one.

The scream of sirens was getting closer now, and soon there would be nowhere to run or hide. He grabbed Sara by the arms and took her into the house. They progressed down some stairs and into a deep cavern-like room. It was like an underground warehouse. Judas did not exist in this world and so, each time he wanted to escape, he could enter his world where he could not be touched or harmed. His body would seem to be here, taking blows, but it was just a mirage—an illusion—like everything else in this make-believe world.

It was common for the killers to enter the wormhole to find their mate; sometimes they were successful, whilst other times they were not. Judas knew he had found her: it took him a while to discover and admit it, but now he recognised he needed to finish the job.

He could hear them in the distance: the marines were coming to take him home before he could get to the wormhole, but he refused to be stuck here, cleaning up jobs. They would have to come to his world and face him there. This would be his last fight.

It didn't matter if they won: he would let them see what they came to see, and then he would be gone. He would carry the cross forever for her if she did not make it. Now, it was safe, but not for long. They were coming—and so was the wormhole. He was going home.

Judas set his watch and watched as the seconds counted down. He would leave the earth through the only door he knew existed, and he would journey to his home, which was not as dark or deadly as this one. It was an earth where the body could choose to die or to go on living, where cells could renew and knowledge was already held, and by their sheer will to stay alive, cells would renew on their own—a miracle in nature. There, you could heal your cells. It was a method of thought, a choice. Everyone in the earth could see this but refused to help. Instead, killing to survive was a way of life, targeting their unseen enemies. They viewed wars as a means to an end.

Judas explained all of this to Sara, and pleaded with her to journey with him. 'Sara, we are so close now. Please don't walk away.'

Covering her ears, Sara walked away, shouting at Judas. 'You are the worst liar I have ever met!'

Judas was weary, and a sad expression fell across

his face. He could not hold back what he was feeling; he had to show her the wormhole. Her gift would allow her to see it, and then at least she could see he was not a liar. 'I can prove it,' he said angrily, hurting knowing how much she was scared to know the truth of who and where she came from and where she belonged.

His heart was on fire for her. He could see that if he stayed in this world with her, as she wanted, he would need to die with her. And if she chose that, he must remain in her arms. It was home for him. He would need to create and help bridge time with another realm of existence, but his mind was not focused. He willed it to open—a skill his elders at his home had mastered, but they were trained to use it, and only in emergencies, such as when a disaster was pending in a country where millions were about to die. Judas, however, was not trained for that mission. He was sent to find the gifted ones, who could save some of the gifted—like Sara. Then returning to the future would be worth it. This was their only purpose to hold it open long enough or their worlds would collide though time and be destroyed and eaten up by an endless cycle of entering one wormhole and then another and another, continuously, with time keeping it this way. If they were to keep it open long enough, the time lapse would no longer exist in their world.

He could not let her go above now—it was too dangerous. Judas knew he wanted to show her the way out, more than ever. His thoughts were blocked and the wormhole was getting closer: he could feel its pull. It was also distorting Sara's thoughts: she could not see the future of events that were close to her heart. The confusion was too much for her: Judas did not realise the danger. She shattered and crumbled in tears, hugging herself on the floor.

'Go away, Judas! I don't want to kill you anymore! I admit I did but my mission to find you and kill you is over nothing…. I want you to go far away from me when they come. Please do as I say just this once. They can take me, as it is me they will want. I can live with that. But I can't live with the thought that you were my job— my assignment. Now I can know you were my last job. They told me no more. They said I could go on and write all about the closed red files, but I see now it was a trap to get us both here. They were ahead of me. My doubts clouded my visions. I would never know something that makes you seen less and less a liar.'

As tears ran down her face, realisation took over her expression, and fear disappeared, quickly replaced with a sad look. 'We have thirty minutes to decide who lives and who walks away.' She pointed her gun in his face, her hands trembling. She stepped back nervously, like a broken toy. She wept, looking at him in his eyes. But she knew something was wrong, and it was coming her way. Someone dear to her heart was going to die, but she had no choice. She was seeing it all. Why was she sent to do a job? To find a killer who eluded her? He was responsible for the killing of her marine boyfriend. She could see herself playing in a garden, a pink sky overhead with two red glowing moons—the earth she came from. But she could not accept this truth of another earth-like planet. Nonetheless, she could not go back: she had been brought here to do a job, and to finish it here, to die here, was her destiny. She had to finish it: the voice in her head kept telling her it was all a lie. And then her body felt an electric shock.

Suddenly, she could not think; she was frozen with fear.

'Don't you think you should have believed me?' Judas asked.

The go 19 was light to carry in Sara's hands, but suddenly it felt weighty. She let go as he commanded through his thoughts. His power was arrestingly and alarmingly stronger than her; his mind was trained and was not easily distracted by anything right now.

Judas was a mind controller. He knew how to get a mind to do exactly as he wanted it to. He did not come from this world; he was a hybrid human from a more advanced world. He was sent here from the future. Sara had fallen dangerously in love with this killer, and although he was only that to her, she admitted she wanted all of him in her life.

He passionately kissed her tears away as he lifted her from the ground and into his arms. She let go and let him guide her; she wanted all of this man. He needed her love and she would rather die in his arms than let go of him now.

He carried her up the stairs and headed towards the hills and up to the sky. Outside was silent, and there was a tornado-like opening where stars were blinking and flashing like a window into space. A

'Judas, where are you taking me? I can't go to your world with you. That world is your destiny, not mine.'

'No, Sara, it is both ours now. We are one. We are no longer split apart.'

'Are you for real? Do you think I believe in that stupid thing they call soulmates?'

Looking down, Sara quickly pulled the gun from her waist and fired a shot into the distance. Two of the agents—men in black—had found them. The other two had been sent from China to finish the job themselves, but they were distracted by the wormhole. Nevertheless, they regained their focus and were relentless in their pursuit to cover up the spilled red files that killed over a million villagers and the red dead springs. This was no longer a fight for Judas or Sara to win; the US government was not giving the facts. The files vanished; the real files were now on Sara's USB drive. Hunters were firing guns from behind the officers. A lone sniper killed all four.

Sara could see another Judas walking towards them: his twin brother. They were identical; except for his limp, he was the image of Judas. He hugged his brother tightly and told him to go and not return. He looked at Sara. 'You both don't belong here anymore. Forget this mission. It is over. We will take care of the rest. This is your chance to escape, Sara. You never belonged here— even if you don't remember where you really came from, your home is now with Judas. He will take care of you.'

Sara nodded. 'I feel as though I have met you

before…'

'You will see, we all have a twin in different times and realms. I came to replace Judas—that is all you need to know for now. Soon, all of this will be gone, and your memory will only remember this world as a world of endless wars, where love like yours would never survive if you both were to stay here.' The twin turned and walked away.

'I don't want to know what just happened or who he is…' Sara whispered tenderly. 'I've had enough for one day. Maybe it is time we chose our next ride out of here—together.'

Judas took Sara in his arms. Her dark eyes searched his as he leaned into her and kissed her fully on the mouth.

CHAPTER ELEVEN: HOME

'What are you afraid of, Sara?'

'What am I afraid of?' Sara repeated with annoyance. 'You are the one that kept this from me until now! Your impatient watch checks... I should have known it was all a trap!'

'What are you talking about, Sara?' Judas pleaded, as he entered their hideout, which was decorated with Spanish cultured tiles, bright orange and red furniture, books everywhere, displayed in the ceiling-high oak shelves.

'I guess I am not the only one that loves ancient reads.'

'No, you are not, babe. I am an avid collector. I mean, my brother—who you met briefly—lived in this house.' Judas threw his arms up in the air and walked up towards the airy porch. He was running out of time: in less than twenty minutes, the wormhole would disappear and his home would be gone. He would be stuck here, but it was worth it he now he had someone to share his life with. She was hot and willing to try everything in the book.'

His arms caged her as she entered the room. 'You are afraid of yourself. I have seen what you can do with the mind. At least I have learnt to control my talent.' Judas lit her fire; he liked her this way.

'Maybe it's evil and not meant to be used,' she suggested. 'Anyway, important things first: we must go visit the London Museum of Arts…'

'Why, Sara?'

'It is where I hid the files when I last visited. The files are there, behind the paintings of the famous Edgar Allen Poe, the poet. I knew they would be safe there. I could be wrong but I can sense the files are still there, waiting for the British government to do something about the pollution cover-up in China, exposing the key silent players. I know this is nothing compared to another earth with a doorway on a timer, allowing passage through a wormhole—although that sci-fi stuff belongs in books and movies.'

'Forget it, Sara. We don't have the time to go to London. Don't worry; it will be safe in London. We will in the future, but now we have a decision to make.'

She jerked away from him. He wrapped both arms around her slender waist and pressed kisses down her neck, and she responded by pressing herself against his rock-hard bulging cock.

'I know I should have protected you and told you the truth. I am sorry.' He could not bear to lie to her. He inhaled her fragrance and felt the silk of her hair against his face. Her long hair was everywhere. He was shirtless now. His chest was covered with bullet wounds and scars; it was like a battlefield. His body told tales of one man's war with his internal demons. She wanted him right then and there, as he bent his head and kissed her. He could kiss her forever like this. He undressed her; he was on fire for this magical woman who was wrapping him up in sex and murder.

His cock felt like steel, and he slammed it into her, disappearing into her hot depths. He drew in his breath as Sara moaned, rocking back and forth with every hot stroke. She held on, wrapping her long, beautiful legs around his legs and backside, letting go and giving herself in to his wild loving.

This mysterious man, from nowhere, was stealing her heart. This killer of this world was her soulmate.

Pure, raw passion, coiling in their hearts, encouraged them to succumb. Their fiery heat was weakening their bodies, causing them to collide into each other, with waves of shocking orgasm stealing their hearts. 'Let go, my angel, and fly with me.' Judas collapsed into her arms. Her body was bucking helplessly as his seed spilled like milk over her thighs, her body flushed. They made love on the Mexican rug on the floor of the towing library sitting room—the room welcoming guests upon entering the house. Now, the wormhole was waiting, and Judas pulled Sara off the rug, shirtless, and dragged his jeans on quickly. He held his shotgun as Sara quickly pulled on her t-shirt and jeans.

'No, Judas, I am not leaving with you.'

Judas smiled and pointed the gun to his head. 'See you on the other side, my angel. Come to me quickly.'

The deafening blow of the gunshot sent Judas's body to its knees. His brains splattered across the rug. The books fell onto the floor, his blood trickling slowly where the bible and Quran fell together, next to one another, each becoming drenched in his blood.

Sara poured over him and took his head into her hands. She was in utter shock. She could not have seen it: he had blocked her thoughts. She screamed his name in torment. At that very moment, Judas's brother fired one shot from the open doorway, hitting Sara directly in her broken heart, causing it to explode. She saw it coming but she had given in to the final task, calling death, as she willingly and painlessly collapsed onto Judas's chest, blood pouring from her mouth as she fell. She felt her body fall light as a feather, and reached out for Judas's hands.

In their new world, he reached out to her, smiling in the glimmering sunlight of his world. It was the most peaceful sight, and she was home now—in his arms, in his world.

'Sara, I told you there's one way out. I lied: there was and is always a choice to find the other way out together.'

Sara smiled and gazed up at his angelic, glowing face. 'I guess there was more than one way out.' She looked up at the starlit skies with its two full moons. She was bathed in light, and her surroundings were light with a soft glow, twinkling lights following their every step. They were on a sandy beach where the horizon was glowing with stars. She pointed in the direction of the star that was drawing her attention.

'Until our next mission... I always wanted to visit London in the spring.' She smiled and rested her head against the man from her dreams.

Judas smiled as they walked on into their mission.

'We shall be there in time to have tea.'

Sara burst into laughter.

'Snarls of love will find us—again.' He pointed to the wormhole in the sky. 'It dares us to fall in love.'

'Oh, Judas. Always the poet. You amaze me,' she said tenderly as she kissed him.

She remembered that time meant nothing here. This was a world where time did not exist. But regardless, her heart melted for him and all they would share.

THE END

www.ingramcontent.com/pod-product-compliance
Lightning Source LLC
Chambersburg PA
CBHW071326130626
46556CB00004B/1774